DATE DUE

D1172958

Captain Hawaii

Captain Hawaii

Anthony Dana Arkin

HarperCollins*Publishers*

Captain Hawaii
Copyright © 1994 by Anthony Dana Arkin
All rights reserved. No part of this book may be used or reproduced
in any manner whatsoever without written permission except in the
case of brief quotations embodied in critical articles and reviews.
Printed in the United States of America. For information address
HarperCollins Children's Books, a division of HarperCollins
Publishers, 10 East 53rd Street, New York, NY 10022.

Library of Congress Cataloging-in-Publication Data
Arkin, Anthony Dana.
   Captain Hawaii/ Anthony Dana Arkin.
      p.   cm.
   Summary: While vacationing in Hawaii, fifteen-year-old Arron be-
comes involved with a tour guide, his beautiful daughter, and a ruth-
less developer who seeks an ancient secret hidden on the island of
Kauai.
   ISBN 0-06-021508-9. — ISBN 0-06-021509-7 (lib. bdg.)
   [1. Hawaii—Fiction.   2. Mystery and detective stories.]   I. Title.
PZ7.A6875Cap   1994   94-2683
[Fic]—dc20   CIP
                                                                  AC

Typography by Steven M. Scott
1   2   3   4   5   6   7   8   9   10
❖
First Edition

For Mom and Dad

Captain Hawaii

CHAPTER 1

The day we left for Hawaii, I came home to a house in shambles. It was like wildebeests had been running around inside and then left. My parents have always gone into fits of insanity trying to organize the family vacations, but this time it was worse than ever.

"Arron Pendleton has come home from school!" I shouted, dumping my books on the trash compactor. That's where I always keep them, hoping that someday they might accidentally fall in. I took an apple off the kitchen counter and went in search of my mom and dad.

They were somewhere in the living room, hidden behind a mountain range of clothes, books, cameras, and suitcases. I'd never seen such a mess in my life. It was like they were about to flee the country.

"Arron? . . . " said my father, rummaging under layers of shirts in his garment bag.

My mother was modeling a safari hat in a compact mirror. "Hello," she said. "How do you like this?"

"The hat?" I asked. "Fine. Very you. Aren't you

going to ask me about school?"

"Did something happen?"

"No. It was school. Nothing ever happens at school. I spent the afternoon practicing my hula."

"Hula, eh?" said my father. "Let's see."

"Can't now," I said, heading up the stairs. "Gotta talk to Davey about the temple of doom."

"Have you seen my electric razor, or my blue socks, or my diving watch?" he called from the landing.

"Sorry, no."

"Don't take too long," warned my mother. "We have to leave for the airport in less than an hour."

The temple of doom was what people called my room. It was because of the animals. I have a few of them—parrots, fish, three or four snakes, even a monkey. I've been collecting since I was seven. I'm fifteen now, so that's a lot of collecting. Ever since I can remember I wanted to be a zoologist and an explorer. When I was little I read *National Geographic* or watched nature documentaries while other boys played softball. I loved anything to do with wilderness—except, I should point out, spiders. I don't deal well with arachnids.

Davey Jones was waiting with his toussled hair and his thick glasses. He was only twelve, but he was an honest-to-god genius, and the only human besides myself who wasn't afraid to enter my room. The general feeling about Davey was that he would win the Nobel Prize by the age of twenty-five, but he'd have to change his name first.

I pointed to the three posters hanging above the desk. "Before I let you care for my creatures, Davey, you must name the three people you see hanging up there on the wall. Consider this a test of your worthiness."

Without batting an eye, Davey answered, "Indiana Jones, Jacques-Yves Cousteau, and Elle Macpherson."

"Very good," I said, handing him a box of fish flakes. "You might just become an adventurer yet."

It was some kind of miracle, but eventually we did make it out the door. We had eleven bags stuffed to the bursting point with useless stuff. I think my parents packed everything they owned. My little brother Robby and little sister Tracy had one whole suitcase filled just with stuffed animals and plastic robots.

My other sister Lisa had to bring all her "mature young woman" stuff—she was in college and thought she was better than everyone. She had a whole case of makeup, a shopping bag of heavy-breather novels, and a duffel jammed with girl clothes she would never wear. I brought close to nothing, afraid we'd make the plane too heavy and crash into the Pacific Ocean.

We drove to Kennedy airport in the snow. The flight was a nightmare. Two flights actually, since we had to stop in Los Angeles. The stale air smelled funny, and my alleged chicken dinner was still frozen in the center. We saw one and a half movies—the second one broke down in the middle.

I dozed off at some point and didn't wake up till we were almost on top of Oahu. Sliding up the window shade, I squinted into the morning light. Up ahead were hazy green dots in the water—islands! Actual Hawaiian islands. It even looked like paradise from thirty thousand feet.

Passengers were starting to stretch and order coffee from the steward with his wobbly little cart. Robby yawned in my ear and wanted to play a game of war, but I couldn't pull myself from the window. I just stared down on the place the gods had made on a good day.

Chapter 2

In Honolulu we had to wait an hour for a connecting flight to Kauai, so I bought a guidebook at the gift shop and read some. These are a few things I learned. . . .

There are seven Hawaiian islands. Kauai (pronounced Kuh-why) is the northernmost island. It's small, only about thirty-three square miles, but it's crammed with deserts, mountains, and my favorite—jungles.

In the center of Kauai is Mt. Waialeale, which is actually an old volcano. They say it's dormant, that means sleeping—not dead—but it hasn't blown in thousands of years. Waialeale catches the storm clouds as they roll by, making that mountain the wettest spot on earth. With all that rain, plants grow like crazy. That's how Kauai got its nickname—the Garden Isle.

Kauai's also got a history of folklore and legends that some people take very seriously. King Kamehameha, the great Hawaiian ruler, was never able to conquer the Garden Isle. They say Captain Cook discovered the Hawaiian islands in 1778, but that's stupid since early Polynesians found it long before he ever did. He was just the first white man, or haole, to step foot there. When he first landed on Kauai the natives thought he was a god. On subsequent visits he fell into serious disfavor and they killed him. Hawaii was the last place the great captain ever saw. That gave me plenty to ponder on the jumper flight to the Garden Isle.

The hotel van dropped us off under the overhanging entrance to the Blue Egret Resort Hotel and sped back to the airport for its next load of tourists. Within seconds our bags were whisked away and we were kissed by Hawaiian ladies who loaded us down with flower necklaces.

I couldn't believe what I was seeing. There was a volcano in the driveway that blinked red lights and spat fountains of steam. Giant doors like the portals of a temple opened to the lobby, which was easily the size of a football field. Everything inside was made to look as if you were in Hawaii, which is where you already were. There were trees and lagoons and wooden bridges. There were plastic tiki statues and parrots—even a canoe hanging from the ceiling. It was horrible. My parents loved it.

Once we checked in, the bell captain gave us a map of the resort and explained how to find all the things necessary for survival. It was like a war movie. He circled our rooms with a red pen, then drew routes to the four restaurants, the six bars, the gym, the steam bath, the duck pond, the stores, the tour activities desk, the beach, and the library.

After we unpacked in our rooms, we followed the map to an aqua-pink dining hall and had a much needed lunch. It was there that I realized this vacation might be the worst in history. My whole family had on these tired, mellow expressions. I could see it coming. They weren't going to do anything fun. Not once in the whole week and a half.

Right after lunch they set themselves up by the pool, with books and magazines and drinks and sun block and sunglasses and bathrobes and towels spread out around them like it was Christmas. It was clear this was where they were staying. This might be their idea of a vacation, but it was not mine.

I wandered down by the towel hut and rented snorkeling equipment, but I hardly saw anything down there—too many people messing up the sand and scaring the fish away. The beach was as crowded as the water, and everyone stared disdainfully at my pale skin as I rinsed off under the beach shower and shuffled back to the pool.

My family still showed no sign of moving off their deck chairs. There they sat, microwaving in the sun, moving only to turn a page.

I slouched over to the pool bar, ordered a virgin piña colada and drank it too fast, freezing my teeth and the back of my head. It's depressing hanging around a hotel hoping for something to happen. I felt trapped. I had highway toes: I needed to explore, to have some adventure.

I ate the pineapple the waitress had stuck on the side of the glass, and signed for the drink. Then, wandering to the lobby, I bought a local paper called the *McKraft Examiner* and went up to floor 8, where my room was.

I took off my shoes, fell back on the bed, and turned on the TV. They were showing a "Land of the Lost" marathon—hours and hours of this Saturday morning kids show I used to watch. It was about a family traveling back in time and getting stuck in prehistory, with dinosaurs and guys in lizard suits who were always trying to drag the children into underground homes and enslave them.

I glanced at the headlines in the *McKraft Examiner:*

Mama Kauai Bar Adds on to Lounge

Anthropology Student Still Missing

Woman Claims She Speaks with Pele

I didn't read the paper. Instead, I watched TV and eventually fell asleep, dreaming about "Land of the Lost." It was just the same as the show, only in my dream it was my family stuck in prehistory with dinosaurs, which I thought was an improvement over being stuck by the pool with the Wall Street Journal crowd.

"Adventure!"

Huh?

"Excitement!"

What?

"The thrill of a lifetime!" said the voice from the television. "Try Zodiac Pirate Tours with Daniel Pierce and his experienced crew and have all your South Seas dreams come true!"

CHAPTER *3*

I *was only semiawake* and the TV commercial was jumbled in my brain, but I grabbed a pencil and scribbled down what I'd heard. Adventure. Excitement. Daniel Pierce Zodiac Pirate Tours. Got it.

The ad was not glitzy. No production value, as my dad would say—and he knew, being an advertising man. It was just a grainy photograph of a rubber boat cruising by this craggy, jungle coast. But everybody in the boat looked tan and tough and strong. And most important they looked like they were having fun, which I at the time was not.

I had to go on that ride.

I found the hotel's tourist information desk just as the lady was going off duty, but she cheerfully agreed to stay and help me. She had about a billion brochures and advertisements for every possible activity, and I grabbed handfuls of them, anything that looked fun. Then I found the pamphlet for Captain Dan's Zodiac Adventure tours and asked her to please book me on the next trip.

Suddenly she was less cheerful. She tried to sell me on another company, Stingray Cruises. She said it was expensive but much, much better.

"Thanks," I said, "but I go on hunches. I got a hunch about this Captain Dan Guy."

"Suit yourself," she said, real snooty. For some weird reason she was peeved at me for taking the wrong cruise. But she made the phone call anyway and reserved a place for me the next day, eleven o'clock.

"So, did everyone have fun today?" my father asked as we sat down to a fish dinner at Chateau Blue Egret. Most of us nodded a big yes.

"Oh, I feel like a new woman," said my mom.

"Me too," said Lisa. "I'm totally relaxed. Just wish there was a place to buy some things."

"How about you, Arron," asked Dad. "You're having a good time, aren't you? Not too boring, I hope."

"Oh, no," I said. "I mean, you know me. I've never really been a pool person. As a matter of fact, you know what? I thought I might want to see a little of the island while I'm here."

"Well, you can do that," he said.

"You want to leave the hotel?" asked Robby. He thought I'd gone nuts.

"Well, yah," I told him.

"Everything is here," said Tracy.

"I know, Tracy. It's a nice place. But I'd just like to hike around, see what the island is really like."

"Mom and I are going to an old whaling town on Tuesday. You're welcome to come with us if you like," offered Dad.

"Uh, I don't know," I said. "I had something in mind more . . . "

"Childish?" offered Lisa.

"No. Ambulatory," I said.

"Arron, this is your vacation too," said Dad. "You don't have to sit around the hotel with us.

Take off, do some exploring."

"You wouldn't mind?" I asked.

"Not at all," he said.

"Where are you planning to go?" asked my mom.

"Here," I said, whipping out the brochure. My dad looked at the picture of the little black raft.

"It's not dangerous, is it?" asked Mom, right on cue.

"Oh, Judy, nonsense," said Dad. "It looks like fun, Arron."

"Well, it certainly is beautiful," said my mom.

"Unreal," said Lisa.

Tracy just ate her fish, and Robby told me he thought the boat looked like a deathtrap and that I wouldn't survive the afternoon.

Chapter 4

Early the next morning I caught the shuttle van for Hanalei. It was cramped in there with the other tourists, all of them sunburned and strapped with camera equipment, but I sat by the window and watched paradise speed by. It was amazing. There were waterfalls, steaming rivers, sprawling sugar cane farms. Lots of horses too, and big dusty buffalo with their brown fur molting in the sun.

The van traveled through rustic towns with all

the usual hangouts—ice-cream parlors, pizza joints, beaches. Locals moseyed around in shorts and flip-flops, no cares in the world. Occasionally we'd pass a sprawling shopping mall or one of the monster hotels by the water. But as we went farther north the rain forest took over and I noticed less of the touristy stuff. The road got worse and there were fewer buildings, fewer towns.

Hanalei, the last town on Route 56—which was by now a potholed, two-lane street—was tiny. Just two rows of clapboard buildings housing artsy boutiques and water-sport charter companies. There were two restaurants, the Shell House and the Hanalei Dolphin. The van stopped at the Ching Yung Shopping Village, a small cluster of stores that offered health foods, camping goods, and yoga classes.

I cinched up my day-pack and stepped out of the van into the sunlight. It felt good to be on my way.

"Take it easy, bruddah," said the driver.

"Thanks," I said. "Hey, before you go, could you tell me where to find Captain Dan's Zodiac Pirate Tours? I'm on their eleven-o'clock tour."

The driver shook his head.

"Sorry, no idea, man. But hey, you be careful. That dude's supposed to be crazy. Have a nice day."

He shut the door and sped south, leaving me to find the notorious captain by myself.

14

CHAPTER *5*

What *a disappointment!* Captain Dan's Zodiac Pirate Tours was a beaten-up, weedy, dump of an office, with an old yellow sign hanging crooked above the door. The building sagged. It looked abandoned. Heat and rain had worn it down till the whole place looked soggy.

I went in. The office was empty. When I called out, no one answered. There wasn't even a service bell, but behind the counter was a door, so I opened it and stepped through.

The back room was like an airplane hangar— high ceiling, diesel smells, and oily machines. Light streamed from windows above the big garage doors. Worktables crammed with tools and scuba gear squatted along the back wall. Work lights hung over three big Zodiac rafts resting on their towing platforms. The black rubber looked smooth as dolphin skin.

Two grown men sat in one of the boats. Two grown men dressed completely in pirate clothes: knee-high boots, hooks, tricornered hats—the works. The big pirate was lying back against the inflated side of the boat, one hand behind his head, the other hand holding a rope that went straight up to the ceiling. The older pirate sat up in the bow. He was reading poetry out the side of his mouth, which was almost hidden by a very red and uncombed beard.

"I wanted the gold, and I sought it," he read.

"I scrabbled and mucked like a slave.
Was it famine or scurvy—I fought it;
I hurled my youth into a grave.
I wanted the gold, and I got it—
Came out with a fortune last fall,
Yet somehow life's not what I thought it,
And somehow the gold isn't all."

Suddenly the old pirate looked at me, threw down the book, and scrambled to his feet, screaming bloody murder. The big one glanced up and calmly jerked the rope he was holding.

Before I could think what to do, a fishing net dropped from the ceiling and twisted around me like a python. I tried to escape but my arms and legs got all tangled up in the netting. I then lost my balance, fell backward, bruised my shoulder, and bashed my head on the bottom of the door.

Like a flash the two men were standing over me, barking names like barnacle, and landlubber, and varmint. Then the one with the beard finished by calling me a worthless vandal.

"Now what do you have to say for yourself," he growled.

"Pendleton. Party of one," I said, teeth clenched.

Their faces went pink with shock and horror. They looked so funny it was almost hard to be angry at them. Almost. My head really hurt.

"My G-God, you're a c-customer?!" choked the bearded man.

I spat some fishnet fuzz out of my mouth.

"Not yet," I said. "I'm not a customer yet."

They both knelt down and began untangling me from the net. The big man opened a scrimshaw knife.

"Don't hurt me anymore," I warned.

"No, no, no, just lie still," said the bearded man, as his friend cut me free. "Are you hurt?"

Gently, I felt the back of my skull and was relieved when I didn't touch my brain.

"There!" the big one said, cutting the last string. "How's that? Can you get up?"

I sat up slowly, not sure if I had dislocated anything. I hadn't. No breaks, no blood.

"Come on, Craig," said the older one. "Let's give him a hand up. Easy now. Slowly."

They eased me up and over to a canvas chair. The big one brought me water in a paper cup from the cooler. I drank it in silence while the bearded one squinted at me, like he was trying to mine the secrets of my soul.

"Now how ya' feeling?" he asked.

"Fine. I mean, I feel okay. Do you do that to all your customers?"

"Do what?"

"Attack them. Do you normally attack your customers, or did I get a bonus?"

The bearded one laughed nervously. "So you're Mr. Pendleton," he said, sweating. "Hahaha, well, it's good to . . . I'm Dan Pierce. Captain Dan Pierce. This is my partner, Craig. I'm sure glad you got a sense of humor. Hoo, gee whiz. I can't tell you how sorry we are, but I think we can explain. I think."

Craig got up with disgust and went into the front office.

"See, we haven't had much business lately—"

"We haven't had any business lately!" hollered Craig.

"And you're the first customer we've had in nearly two weeks."

"We forgot what customers look like, that's why we didn't recognize you," said Craig, coming back with coffee and a jelly doughnut. Bored with me, he picked up some papers and tried to organize them.

"Boy oh boy, what a boo boo we made," laughed the captain. "That was really dumb-ola."

"Yeah. See, we thought you were a spy," said Craig, jelly dripping out of the doughnut and onto his clipboard.

"A spy?" I said.

"Yeah. Have you ever heard of industrial espionage? We thought you were spying for Stingray Cruises."

"Let me handle this," snapped Captain Dan. "You're confusing the heck out of him. See, we're kind of in a war with Stingray Cruises. They're this other Zodiac company and they've got a lot of money and fancy equipment and they think they're just God's gift to pleasure boating—"

"Now who's confusing him?" said Craig.

"Give me a break, will you? Where was I? Where . . . ?"

"Stingray Cruises," I said.

"Indeed. Basically, they stink. They're eating up all the little boat companies—"

"Ate them," corrected Craig.

"Ate 'em, yes. Ate almost everybody but us. But we're fighting back. We are not just going to sit back and let them win, no sir. Would you? Would you do that?"

"No, I guess not . . ." I said.

"Of course you wouldn't. Not if you were me. Not if you'd been here longer than anybody!" said the captain, getting worked up now. "For crying out loud, my brother Craig and I started this here business nearly twenty years ago. . . . But that's not the point, is it?"

"The point," said Craig, "is that for the last two

months it's been out and out war. Sabotage, vandalism, all kinds of underhanded things."

"So you figured I was working for Stingray Cruises and came by to put sand in your gas tank, or something?" I said.

"Yes," said Captain Dan. "Hey, that's not a bad idea. Craig, make a note of that. Sand in the gas tank."

"We've done that one already," said Craig.

"Well gee, I'm sorry," I said. "It sounds very . . . uhh . . ."

"Hey, listen, that's the way it goes. Keeps me young." The captain actually sounded sad and old. "Anyway, our luck is changing, isn't it? We got a customer today, right?"

He leaned over and patted me on the shoulder, my bad shoulder, the one I fell on. I smiled through the pain.

"Still want the eleven-o'clock tour, don't you? It's a beautiful day."

"I don't know . . ." I said.

"Oh, come on, sure you do! You know you want to."

"It's an awfully good day for it," coaxed Craig, jamming the last of the doughnut into his mouth. "Would it make you feel any better if you weren't the only passenger going?"

"I suppose it would," I said.

"We'll get 'em!" said the captain. "Craig, you try

and rustle up some more folks. Try anything. There's gotta be someone in town you can find. Then, Mr. Pendleton, we'll get some sandwiches, some chow, you'll see some sights, meet the rest of my crew. It'll be a day you'll never forget. I promise. What do you say?"

"Hmmm."

"Come on, you're no wimp, are you? You're no dumb run-of-the-luau tourist. You're made of tougher stuff than that! Of course you'll come."

"Well . . ." I said realizing no adventurer worth a flat dollar would ever back out now. "Well, yes. You bet I'll come."

CHAPTER 6

Still *dressed like pirates*, the captain and Craig went over to the Ching Yung Shopping Village to grab some unsuspecting tourists for the eleven-o'-clock tour.

"Why are you dressed like pirates?" I had asked before we left the hangar.

They had admitted that their costumes might look strange—the big feathery hats and velvet pants—but the two brothers explained these props were for the new brochure they were designing. Business was so bad, they decided to do a new campaign with a photo of the crew dressed as buccaneers. The costumes had arrived that morning, and the fellows were trying them on when I appeared. It made sense to me, but I wondered about the unsuspecting tourists.

I had a job to do as well. The captain had given me a list and asked if I would run across the street to the Tropical Deli and pick up lunch. "Sea chow," as he called it. It was the strangest list I'd ever seen.

4 Sunburst Special
2 Pele Turkey
1 Paniolo Grill
1 Sushi du jour
1 Menehune Malted w/ sprout roll
P.S. Ask Kate for the usual extras.

There was still a doubt in the back of my mind about how smart it was to go on the trip. I mean, being attacked by your captain is not an ideal way to start an ocean voyage. There was always the possibility that he was very crazy—not bad, just crazy—and the idea of getting lost at sea with him as my only chance for survival was not comforting.

Maybe I could still get my hard-earned sixty-five dollars of baby-sitting money back. It wasn't too late. I was sure there were other tours and plenty of other captains in town. More reputable captains. Safer ones. Maybe Stingray Cruises wasn't such a bad idea after all.

But as I stood in front of the Tropical Deli thinking all this through, a girl carrying a crate of tools came out and went around the back of the building. She was wearing a carpenter's apron. As she walked by, panther spots of light and shadow slid across her in shifting patterns. She looked proud. She was incredible, the kind of girl that made a guy pray for a natural disaster so he could save her life and be brave.

Who was I kidding, I thought? Just go in and buy the lunch.

CHAPTER 7

Right away I smelled trouble. Inside the deli, a guy in a Stingray Cruises T-shirt was rubbing his stomach and mumbling, "Come on, baby, light my fire." He was drunk and he couldn't carry a tune.

No one was there to wait on us. The girl was probably still in the backyard, so I looked around the store. It wasn't a DELI deli but more like some cosmic sushi–health bar, with tasty-looking nutrifood chilled behind glass. Above the counter hung a chalk board with the menu and specials written out in a rainbow of colors. Under that was the motto Food for the Body and Spirit.

The Stingray guy was impatient. He kept hitting the service bell and saying, "Hey! Hey man . . ." He really had been drinking.

"I'll be there in a second," called the girl, and soon she was standing behind the counter, dusting off her jeans. She was even prettier up close.

"Sorry to keep you waiting," she said to Stingray.

"Don't worry about it, man," he said lazily, like he was draining sea water out of his sinus. He shoved his Saran Wrapped sandwiches and soda bottles toward the cash register.

"Will that be all?" asked the girl.

He sort of snorted and sneered at her. "Unless you want to take off early."

"No, thank you. I've got to work," she said cheerfully, ringing up his order.

"Come on, baby, what do you say? The breakers are, like, killer. I know a really cool spot . . . "

"I appreciate it, but I've got to work." She was now a little less cheerful. "That'll be eight dollars and fifty cents."

The surfer grabbed her wrist. "You work too much, maybe."

I was watching this from behind an aisle of corn chips. I realized the situation was getting, as they say, out of hand. Pretty soon I'd have to do something. But what? The guy was very tan and very tall and if he wasn't exactly a hulk, he could easily smash me badly.

"Let go," said the girl.

"Aw, be nice," said the surfer.

I waited a moment to see if maybe the whole thing might die down by itself. Coward, I thought. Here's that natural disaster you were wishing for. It's a perfect way to introduce yourself.

"Please let go my arm," she said again. "That hurts."

I crept down the aisle to the end of the counter, just behind the surfer. So far he still didn't know I was there. My mind raced after something cool to say. The best I could do was: "Hey. HEY! I'm trying to buy some things here, IF YOU DON'T MIND!!"

The guy spun around and peered at me through drunk and beady eyes. They were dark and unfocused, which meant he was hopefully too out of it to break any of my important parts.

"It's okay, brah," he said, waving his hands. "Chill down."

"You chill down," I said. "I'm in a hurry. Now why don't you pay and just get out of here."

He stared at me for a few painful seconds while he tried to figure if I was worth fighting with—or if the girl was worth fighting over. Well, the girl was certainly worth it, that was obvious. That left only me to consider. He's going to kill you after all, I thought. He will boogie-board on your head.

Before he could reach any decision, a van pulled up in front of the deli and honked twice. It had hideous orange flames painted over the hood and doors. It was the perfect van for Stingray.

He gave me the toughest look he could muster, as if to say, "You're just lucky I don't have the time to stay and make you sorry you were born." Then he put ten dollars on the counter, took his food, and snorted his way out to the van. It sped off, leaving me and the girl to begin.

"May I help you?" she asked, as if nothing happened.

I tried to steady my shaking legs. Then, when I had enough breath to speak, I said, "Is he gone?"

"Him? Oh, sure," she said. "Don't worry about him. Do you want to order something?"

"I thought he was going to kill me. I felt my life coming to an end."

"Then why did you yell at him?"

"Well . . . because of you." I was hurt that my bravery had gone unnoticed. "It looked like he was going to hurt you."

"Hurt me?"

"He was twisting your arm, he was drunk. . . . Sorry for butting in."

"He's come in here like that once a week for over a month now. I've gotten used to it. I don't really think he's dangerous."

"Looked it to me. Anyhow, are you all right?"

"Oh, sure." She was wiping down the counters with a sponge. "I've got protection in case of emergency."

"Protection? Like a gun?"

"No." She laughed. "Spartacus." She whistled toward the stockroom. A chain clinked in the backyard and Spartacus appeared in the doorway. He stared at me suspiciously, his massive head tilted to the left. He was a brown pit bull terrier with a barrel chest and jaws like the hinge on a bank vault.

"Pit bull," I said. "I love pit bulls."

"You know dogs?" asked the girl.

Spartacus approached sideways, kind of grinning a sloppy dog smile. I held out my hand and he kissed the ends of my fingers.

"Good dog," I said. "He's great."

"He likes you. He hardly likes anyone. So, can I get you something to eat? It's on the house since you tried to save my life."

I gave her the lunch list and told her where I'd gotten it. I told her I was going on an expedition with Captain Dan, but that I probably shouldn't because I thought he was crazy.

"He's my father," the girl said, studying the list.

I couldn't believe it. It was impossible. No man crazy as the captain could have a daughter as lovely as this.

"I—I'm sorry, I—" I stammered.

"Don't worry about it. Nobody knows better than me how crazy he is."

"I see your point," I said, ashamed of myself.

She was about to start the order when she stopped and stared out the door.

"Duck," she said quickly.

"What?"

"Duck. Get down on the floor, here behind the counter. I think our friend is coming back again."

"But I don't—"

"I'm not kidding. Please hurry, come here."

I don't know how she knew. I didn't hear the van till seconds later when it screamed to a stop outside and the beer bottle, hurtling out the passenger door, smashed through the front window of the Tropical Deli. It burst in and sprayed the floor with glass.

A guy coming down the street stopped to holler at the van as it shot away. He looked sadly at the broken window, then sauntered into the deli and shook his head at the chunks of window that were all over the place.

"Doc!" said the girl, jumping up from behind the counter.

"Can you believe this? They did it again, those jerks."

"Hei," said the man. He was Japanese. "Who's that?" He was pointing at me.

I had my head down under a folding chair, like in an air raid. "Hi. I'm just a customer."

"You poor thing," said the girl, peering under

28

the table where I crouched. "Are you okay? Did you get hit?"

"No, no. I'm fine." I backed up and brushed some glass slivers out of my hair. When I stood up, Doc squinted at me.

"Hmmm," he said.

"Hmmm?" I asked.

"Exciting."

"A little too exciting."

"Hmmm," he said again, looking so closely into my eyes I thought he'd see inside my head. "I've been expecting you. Thought you were taller."

I looked over at the girl, but she was sweeping up, seemingly paying no attention.

"You're probably thinking of someone else," I said. "I didn't even know I was going to be here at all until ten minutes ago. It's all kind of an accident. I just came to pick up a lunch order."

"Hmmm." He rubbed the back of his neck. "There's no such thing as an accident. Good to see you anyway. Been waiting a long time, no?"

"No. I mean, yes, I suppose. But really, I think you're expecting a different person—"

"Sorry, no more talking today. I gotta make sushi."

He clapped his hands and rubbed them together, then went behind the counter and put on an apron. He started to organize his small kitchen, unwrapping raw fish and washing a sinkful of white rice. I didn't have a single clue what he was talking about, and there was this funny pause during which the girl cleared her throat, but no one said anything. It was all kind of weird.

"Wow," I said after the funny pause, looking at the jagged window. Then I said it again. "Wow."

"There's never a dull moment around here," said the girl, emptying a dustpan full of glass into a paper bag. "Doc, we're gonna have to board up this window before tonight."

Doc nodded. "Hei. I'll do it, don't worry."

"Can I help?" I asked. "The tour doesn't leave for another half hour."

"Yes," said the girl. "I mean, if you want to."

Want to? I thought. Want to? I'd crawl through ten miles of swamp to clean up that broken glass.

"Well, yeah, okay. Sure," I said.

This vacation wasn't turning out so pathetic after all.

CHAPTER 8

Her name was Kate Pierce and I helped her make sandwiches. I trailed her around the kitchen and followed her orders as best I could, slicing tofu, toasting bread, blending sprouts. We didn't talk much on account of how busy we were, but I did tell her about how her father and uncle nearly beat me up.

Kate was horrified, but Dr. Gomasio couldn't take it seriously. He laughed till he cried as he chopped squid with a cleaver. Captain Dan seemed to have a reputation around these parts.

Soon the food was boxed and bagged and I had to go back to the Zodiac office to catch a ride to the river. I was excited about the trip but also reluctant to leave the deli, worried that I wouldn't see these people again. I liked Doc and I really, really liked Kate.

While I was thinking all this, Dr. Gomasio patted me on the shoulder and asked how long I would be on the island.

"A little over a week," I said.

"You work good," said Doc. "Do you want a job?"

"You're kidding," I said. "I'm only here a few days. . . . You can't do that."

"Sure he can, he owns the place." said Kate.

"Hei," Doc said. "You want it or not?"

I gave it serious consideration for about two seconds. A paying job where I'd get to spend the day with this girl? Yes. Yes.

"When do I start?"

"You already started," he said.

"Okay, great," I said, grabbing the food and heading for the door. "I'll see you tomorrow."

Big Craig gave me a ride to the Hanalei River, which was really not much of a river, more like a stream. It was where the expedition started from. He was very chummy and apologized again for all the rough business earlier that morning. I told him not to worry about it. I was in a good mood, and why not? Kate Pierce seemed to like me.

Craig parked in the dirt, and I took the bags of food down to where the twenty-foot Zodiac was tethered. There was a fishing boat named *Gilligan* a few yards downriver. *Gilligan*'s captain sat on the shore in an aluminum folding chair, his cap pulled down over his eyes. He was either angry or asleep or both. His T-shirt said Na Pali Cruises.

Captain Dan saw me and rushed over. He'd changed out of his Captain Hook costume and I didn't recognize him until I heard his unmistakable voice. He had the volume up just a little too high, all the time. At close range it caused slight pain.

"There you are, Mr. Pendleton," he said, milking the "Mr." for all it was worth. "Boy, are you a good omen. Three new customers in the space of two hours. Not bad, eh? Some people bring fair weather, you bring customers. I like that." He slapped me on the back like we were buddies from World War II.

I handed him the food. "All I brought is groceries, Captain. Here you go. They were out of mango, so they gave you a papaya shake instead. Everything else is just like you ordered."

"Good, good," he said, peering down into the recesses of the brown bags. "How's my daughter today? Quite a gal, ain't she?"

"Lovely. Store I mean. Really, really nice place. Clean and uhh . . . just, well . . . just a fine place. And your daughter is fine. She seems very nice."

Captain Dan looked at me, suddenly serious.

"Nice, eh?" he said softly. "Listen. You so much as touch her, so help me—"

"I—I—I." I said.

He saw the shock in my eyes and laughed. "It was a joke! I was kidding. Relax! Actually, I should try and set you up with Kate. She doesn't have a boyfriend, never gets out, never socializes, you know? You two should go to dinner, down on the south shore. Maybe she'd take half a day off from work or something. She really needs a break. What do you say?"

"Well, I . . . "

"Just a thought. Take your time deciding. Okay, let's get this show on the road."

He grinned at me and walked back to his pickup truck.

The three customers were a man and a woman and their eight-year-old son. They looked dazed, like maybe they'd been hit over the head and kidnapped and woke up to find themselves going on a

Zodiac Pirate Tour. I realized that could be very close to the truth. They definitely weren't dressed for the occasion. Way too fancy. Lot's of jewelry.

The mother was slathering sunscreen on the boy by the quart. He was squirming and obviously didn't want to be there.

"My parents were s'posed to take me to Disney World and Epcot Center, but they didn't."

"I'm sorry. That's too bad," I said.

"Were you at Epcot Center?" he asked, squinting up at me, kicking dirt with his foot.

"No, I never went there. It's supposed to be fun."

"Sure is," he said. "Not like this. This place stinks. Do you like it here?"

"Actually, I do."

He snickered.

"Pretty stupid!" he said, running over to hide behind his father's legs.

"Forgive him; he's a little hyper," said his mother.

"Oh, it's fine. I have a little brother about his age, I know what it's like," I said, suddenly thinking fondly of Robby, who was pretty cool for a nine-year-old.

"Do you know anything about boats?" she asked.

"Not a whole lot," I said.

"Humphrey's never been in a boat before, but he gets motion sick in cars and elevators. I just hope he doesn't throw up or something." She laughed.

"Honey, he'll be fine. Nothing will happen," said her husband. He turned to me and smiled. "Heh. Kids. Hi, Arnold Norman. This is my wife, Stella."

I shook their hands as Humphrey boasted, "I betcha I throw up on that boat. I betcha ten dollars." I made a mental note not to sit next to Humphrey under any conditions.

Soon the rest of the crew was there, and we were all introduced. Of course there was Dan and Craig—the Corsican Brothers—but Craig went back to the office to do the books. That left Joanne and Terry. Joanne was the only woman in the crew, but she looked tough enough for professional wrestling. She gave us a shaka wave, thumb and pinky only.

Terry was a wiry Australian who said "aloha" like "aylowhah." He wore an enormous floppy hat that had probably belonged to an ex-girlfriend, and ancient, ripped-up surf trunks. That was all.

While this motley bunch inspected the Zodiac and organized the snorkel gear, our captain ran through all the important rules for riding in the rubber boat.

"Just hold on, that's about it," he said, grinning

at his small group of passengers. "It couldn't be simpler. Put your feet under the straps on the deck and hold on to the ropes along the side. If you fall in, we'll swing around and get ya."

"When are we getting in the goddam boat?" whined Humphrey. He was throwing rocks at the raft, bouncing them off the rubber tube. One ricocheted and hit Terry in the knee.

"Better not to do that, son. You might hurt somebody," said Captain Dan.

"I'm just throwing them in the water," said the kid, who pitched a handful that went pelting into the engines.

"Hey, be careful," said Craig.

"Ever been on a boat before, son?" asked Captain Dan.

"Boats are boring," said the kid.

Getting into the raft was awkward, but we managed. The only one who couldn't make it on his own was Mr. Norman. Captain Dan had to push him in by the back end of his safari shorts. I got in without causing a scene.

Dan was about to climb in when a stranger came around the bend. He waved to us and walked down the riverbank. He was strong-looking, but he had a fat stomach and his surfer sunglasses were too small for his tanned face. His thin, greasy brown hair was swept back and hung to his shoulders. He wore a faded Hawaiian shirt, swimming trunks, no shoes, and he carried a watertight, plastic briefcase. The kind that floats.

He asked to come with us and handed Dan a plastic film canister with three crisp twenty-dollar bills and one five rolled inside.

"Well, usually we ask for a day's notice," said Dan, "but since you're paying cash, what the heck. Welcome aboard, Mr. . . . ?"

"Smith," said the new passenger, as he climbed easily into the Zodiac.

Happy as Dan was for another customer, I could tell he was uncomfortable. Something about the stranger bothered him, and although I didn't know exactly why, it bothered me too.

Captain Dan started up the growling engines.

"Just tuck your feet under—" he began, but the stranger interrupted.

"No need for the routine, Captain," he said. "I am quite familiar with these babies." His smile was big and fake under his mirrored bug-eyed glasses. I sat as far from him as possible when we headed out to sea.

CHAPTER 9

"Ahh, *there it is*," said Captain Dan, twenty minutes into our ride. "The Na Pali Coast. Not a bad view is it?"

No, not bad at all. It was fantastic, enormous, amazing in every way something could be amazing. Colors dripped out of the bright landscape and danced on your eyes.

We were quiet. With the engines off the boat was quiet. Only the waves make sounds against the raft, like a dog licking milk. Captain Dan took off his T-shirt and then his hat. So did I. Humphrey shot me a snotty look for kissing up to the captain.

We had been sailing east for about ten minutes, fast over the Pacific. The ride was bumpy and loud. I was thrilled. Captain Dan kept howling, standing at the wheel platform, the wind fluttering his beard like the gills of a fish. The howling took us all by surprise, especially the Normans, who were looking more pinched and uptight every second we sailed away from civilization. But to me the captain's enthusiasm was infectious.

I took huge breaths, my lungs exploding with crisp, briny air. I crawled up to the charging bow and wrapped the wet ropes around my hands. Each time the raft hit a wave it leapt a little into the air, then it would come down hard, slamming the foamy water and spraying the heck out of me.

Wind tunneled through my shirt, swept inside my sunglasses, and banged against my eyeballs, making them tear and squint. If this didn't make you feel alive, you needed an ambulance.

But now we were still and silent, Na Pali

staring us down. Its mountains sprang up from the fishy depths like green crystal skyscrapers, amazingly sharp and pointy. Huge valleys yawned out from the hills and rolled down to the miles of lazy beaches. The rows of peaks near the coast sparkled in the sun like shark's teeth, and the far away ones were lost in creeping mist.

After a minute Captain Dan fired up the Zodiac again and we were off, banging over the rough water, moving fast away from the modern world.

The mouth of the sea cave loomed like the entrance to a nightmare fun house. Its black roof was thirty feet above the water, and it tunneled straight back into the mountain. Inside there was no light.

A stream of water fell from the upper lip of the cave and splashed in front of the entrance. Mr. Norman took four pictures of it from the same angle, smearing sunscreen on his camera with his nose.

"Was this dynamited out," he asked Captain Dan, "or did you find it like this?"

The stranger, Mr. Smith, snickered to himself.

"Better answer the man, Terry," said the captain.

"It's a natural formation, sir," said Terry. "It's called a lava tube. It was created by the volcano thousands of years ago."

Dan faced the raft toward the cave and we idled

there, ten feet from the splashing water. He kept turning around to look behind him and check the wind with his finger.

"Are we going in?" I asked.

"Hold on, Mr. Pendleton," said the captain.

He shoved the throttle and the boat lurched forward, making the Normans yelp. The waterfall was right on top of us and it splashed everyone, especially me.

"Got a little damp there, eh, Mr. Pendleton?" he hollered.

"Just a little, thank you, Captain."

"Well hang on, this'll dry you off."

It was full speed into the blackness of the cave—this time everyone yelped.

"Hold on mateys!" bellowed Terry over the blasting roar of the engines.

I could feel the walls of the cave rushing by, but I couldn't see them. I couldn't see anything. Then Joanne clicked on a searchlight and the tunnel came alive. The rock walls flew by at what seemed like sixty miles an hour. Up ahead the tunnel got smaller and seemed to end abruptly. The Zodiac didn't slow down.

The Normans were crouching low, Mr. Norman pleading for Captain Dan to stop and his wife clutching little Humphrey, who was laughing hysterically at his father. He laughed so hard, he threw up, and not over the side, either.

40

At the last second the captain swerved to the right, whipping the raft under an arch and floating us to rest inside a chamber as big as a house. We were inside the mountain. I heard Captain Dan laugh over the drone of the motors, then he threw his head back and howled, "HOOOWEEEAH-HHH!"

Terry and Joanne did the same. They were wild, like a pack of wolves. I couldn't help myself—"HOOOWEEEAHHH!"—I joined in, adding to the roar till the cave was ringing like a gong. I'm not superstitious, but in that craggy darkness with the cold mist rising and dripping, I imagined ancient spirits shaking their giant heads and rubbing the sleep from their eyes.

CHAPTER *10*

"**J**ust *jump overboard and tow* your stuff behind you on this," said Captain Dan. He held a life vest up in the air for us to see.

We were out of the cave and anchored about two hundred yards off a beach, not a sign of civilization anywhere. I put my sunglasses in my plastic bag that had PENDLE written on it in red marker, grabbed a life vest, and clambered on to the side of the raft. Below I could see coral and fish doing their thing.

Me and Humphrey dove in and paddled around, waiting for the others. They took forever, like grown-ups always do when they're going swimming. Finally they took the plunge and we started for the shore.

I don't know how he screwed up such a simple thing, but Mr. Norman dropped his plastic bag. When it sank to the bottom he yelled out, flailing his arms and breathing in a lungful of water. Then he coughed like he would die. Captain Dan had to swim over and help. He grabbed Mr. Norman under the arms and tugged him over to a life vest where the guy clung like a terrified frog. Terry swam down and salvaged the plastic bag.

I thought Mr. Norman had been bitten by a shark, the way he shrieked and flung his arms around like in *Jaws*. For a second I was really worried, we all were—except for one person.

No one noticed but me because I was next to the stranger when it happened and he'd been careful not to snicker too loud. But I heard him.

"What a jerk," he'd said, and swam on.

We all got to the beach without drowning and climbed onto the pristine sand just like the first creatures that climbed out of the prehistoric stew. I dumped my vest and bag near some rocks at the foot of a sand dune. The beach was wild and beautiful. I'd never seen anything like it in my life before, except on TV, like *National Geographic* or *King Kong*.

"Mr. Pendleton," called my captain.

"Yes, sir?"

"Don't be a stranger, boyo. Come on over here, have a chat."

"All right," I said, and trotted over to Captain Dan and Terry. They were spreading the food out on a ledge at the base of a huge volcanic cliff. It must have been six hundred feet high.

"You're wet," said Captain Dan.

"So it would seem," I said.

"This should help."

He handed me a clean white towel from a stack behind him.

"Kaipo, have you met my friend Mr. Pendleton?"

"Not had the pleasure," said Terry.

"Well here he is. Kaipo, meet Mr. Pendleton. The one worthy customer of the day."

I shook the Australian's hand. "I thought your name was Terry."

"Kaipo's my Hawaiian name. Only my friends use it. You can call me Terry."

This made them howl with laughter. I didn't laugh since I didn't know where I stood with these people. Maybe they were being friendly, but they could also have been ridiculing me like they would any typical, wimpoid tourist.

"Only kidding, mate," said Terry. "You call me Kaipo or any bloody thing you want."

"Kaipo means 'the Sweetheart,'" said Captain Dan. "He likes the ladies and they like him right back. Here, give us a hand. Put the chips into these bowls and take out the paper napkins. Set 'em up over here."

While I worked, Dan shaded his eyes and looked down the beach at the other passengers. He sighed sadly. They wandered around like lost baby chicks.

"What do you think of the new arivee, Mr. Pendleton?" he asked.

"Who? The strange guy, the one who came late?"

"Yeah, the one who came late and just happened to have the exact, full amount in cash down to the penny."

"What should I think of him?"

"Do you like him? Does he make you comfortable?"

"No," I said. "I think he's kind of creepy."

"Creepy is right," said Terry. "He's up to something, that one."

"My sentiments exactly," said the captain. "Mr. Pendleton, if you see him do anything unusual, anything fishy, please report it to me. Would you be so kind as to do that?"

"Okay," I said. The stranger wasn't doing anything fishy now, but he was hunting for shells and he didn't strike me as the shell-hunting type. "Who do you think he is?"

"Ever hear of Stingray Cruises, mate?" asked Terry.

Oh, not this again, I thought. "Yes, I heard of them, but—"

Captain Dan slipped a towering stack of potato chips into his cheek and said, "My bet is he's a spy."

"You think everybody is a spy," I told him. "You thought I was a spy and I'm nothing like a spy. Do you think maybe you're taking this too far?"

Captain Dan smiled at me like I was retarded. "I understand why you might think that," he said, "but I have my ways and reasons, and no, I don't think I'm taking this too far. No, take my word for it, that squeaky bum is a spy. I feel it in my bones and I'm never wrong twice in the same day. Here, have a Maui Potato Chip. It'll do you good."

CHAPTER *11*

I *eyed the stranger for a while,* but he was just getting a tan—nothing unusual in that—so I forgot about it and tried body surfing. Joanne stood on the beach and shouted some pointers. It turned out she had been nearly a champion surfer.

The waves were small by any heavy-surfer-freak standards, but they were big for me. They hauled me under and ploughed my face over the bottom. Soon I was worn out and my skin was sanded raw.

We all gathered for lunch at the base of the cliff, except for the stranger. He took his food and crawled back up the sand dune to sit alone and grimace at the afternoon sun. The rest of us ate health sandwiches, sushi, and potato chips while Mr. Norman went on and on about L.A. real estate, bond trading, and all the things I know nothing about and hope I never do.

Dan and Terry and Joanne had to listen and be nice because that was their job. As tour guides they were paid to talk to the tourists and spread the aloha spirit no matter how boring the tourists might be. I respected their patience, but I had to get out of there or my head would explode from boredom.

"I'd like to take a walk, if that's okay," I asked.

"A walk, eh? Well, that'd be fine," the captain said. "Behind the sand dune is the trail head. That'll take you into the woods. Plenty to see back there, but stick to the trail."

"Thanks, I will," I said and got up to go.

"We're leaving for the next beach in about forty-five minutes, so don't take too much time."

I agreed and trotted off toward the trail that led

steeply up into the thick foliage. It was great to be alone, away from Mr. Norman and Hollywood stories and spies.

Soon the trail leveled off and the forest thinned a little so you could see a few hundred yards ahead. To the left was a bare patch, a little overlook onto the beach. From there I could see the whole bay with the Zodiac anchored in the center, and all the people from the tour lying in the sand. I had climbed higher than I thought.

Mr. Norman was lecturing the crew. The stranger was doing a little snorkeling by the raft, and he still didn't look like he was up to anything. Maybe Dan was wrong about him, I thought. Of course he was wrong. Just because the guy was slimy and unpleasant didn't mean he was a spy, for crying out loud. I decided Captain Dan was paranoid.

I turned around and went farther up the trail above the overlook. I'd been to Yellowstone and Sequoia national parks, but this was real Tarzan country. Towering palms and ferns, huge heart-shaped leaves dripping with dew. The warm, muddy earth smelled like baking bread.

My mind began to wander. I started thinking about Kate Pierce, wondering if it was possible to be in love with someone when you're only fifteen and you've only spent half an hour with the girl making sandwiches. Possible, but unlikely.

Anyway, it was stupid falling for a girl who lived on a tiny island in the middle of the Pacific Ocean, wasn't it?

You can't be romantic and an important scientist. A great explorer would never let a woman interfere with a demanding and dangerous life in the field. Men like Jacques Cousteau and Indiana Jones were unmoved by the ways of love. I had to follow their example. I had to forget about girls.

I had to pee.

I went behind some bushes above the overlook and that was where I was standing, awkwardly, when the stranger appeared.

He trudged up the trail, briefcase in hand, and stopped at the overlook. He did not see me.

He knelt down with the case flat in front of him. He opened it carefully and took out a heavy-duty walkie-talkie, one of those expensive, rubberized jobs. It hissed when he turned it on.

"This is Nihui, do you read?" he said.

"You're late, brah," came the voice on the other end.

"Yeah man, I know," said the stranger. "I'll be up in a second. I'm just testing out my new toy."

"What's that?"

"It's a wicked surprise," he said, reaching back into the shiny briefcase. "Just keep your eye on the bay."

CHAPTER *12*

I *never expected the Zodiac* to explode like that, popping like a balloon out of the water and slapping down in a shredded mess. It floated there in its own oil, a dead jellyfish with two outboard motors.

The stranger put the remote control detonator back in his briefcase. He snickered to himself and rubbed his hands together. The people on the beach were shouting in confusion.

"Oh . . . my . . . gosh," I said, kind of as a reflex and without meaning to.

The stranger heard me and whipped around in surprise.

"You little punk," he said. Then he pulled a knife out of the briefcase—one of those diving knives that cuts through steel and opens giant clams. I couldn't believe it, he had to be joking. I tried to think of something to say, but suddenly he came at me, cursing and pointing the knife. I turned and started running back up the hill.

"Who are you?! Who're you working for?!" yelled the stranger.

"I'm just a tourist, I SWEAR!" I screamed, leaves and branches whipping past my face.

We were both panting from the heat and the running and I quickly realized that I was very lost.

The one thing Captain Dan told me was to stick to the trail, but I'd been so startled that the first thing I did was to run completely off the trail and now it was nowhere to be seen. I was getting more lost with every crazy, frantic leap. I screamed for help, but everyone on the beach was too busy shouting to hear me.

"Stop running, you little jerk! I'm not going to hurt you!"

"Then what's the knife for?!"

He sounded farther away, but I didn't dare turn around to check. Everything was a tangle of vines and scratchy plants; the ground was mud. I put all my concentration inside my feet, on jumping over logs and roots. I tried not to think about getting stabbed in the jungle and left to die. My parents would kill me.

All of a sudden there was a loud crack behind me and an "OWW! @#^$&&$%^*"—the stranger screamed something obscene. I thought he had broken his leg, which would have been fine by me. I turned around but he wasn't there.

"I don't BELIEVE it!" His voice came from somewhere high above me. He was dangling upside down from a rope slung over the highest branch of a tree. A booby trap! A real booby trap that worked, not like the ones I made in the backyard when I was ten. This was a beauty.

His knife lay in the mud. I cautiously walked over and picked it up.

"Cut me loose," he said.

"Are you crazy?" I asked.

"I'm serious, come on. Cut me loose. I won't try anything. I promise."

"I'm just a tourist!" I shouted, angry and shaken. "I have nothing to do with this! Why did you blow up the boat?!"

"Get me out of here and I'll tell you everything you want. Come on. My head's throbbing. Be a good kid."

"You're out of your mind," I said. "How do I get back down to the beach?"

"Why should I tell you?!" he shouted.

"Okay, forget it," I said and left him hanging there. I had always read how a person can get lost very easily in the wilderness. I never believed it. I always thought that if you had even one brain cell in your head you could find some clue, remember some tree or footprint that would remind you where you'd been. Not true. I hadn't been in the woods twenty minutes since I left the beach and nothing looked familiar, nothing looked promising. I began to panic—something else I'd read about but never believed would really happen.

Up ahead I heard the roar of a waterfall, so I ran on. With any luck there would be a lookout, or another trail. But I was out of luck. There was nothing but a scraggly mess of bushes and a two-hundred-foot drop straight down to the water.

Exhausted, I collapsed and slid down into a dark tangle of ferns. My heart raced, my lungs throbbed, and every part of me shook. The knife rattled in my hand.

There had to be a way out, there had to be! I just needed to calm down enough to think. THINK—I thought—THINK! I could go back the way I'd come and risk running into my friend with the briefcase—he'd probably gotten free by now. I could jump into the waterfall and kill myself. Or I could go running up and down, screaming, "HELP ME, HELP ME—YA YA YA!"

I took some deep breaths. Then I made a decision. I would find my way to the bottom of the falls, then follow the stream out to the sea. I stood up.

Men were in the brush, twenty yards above me, the stranger and two new ones. The stranger had a rifle. The second guy was a thug with bulging muscles and tattoos and a crossbow under his arm. The third man was different, a strange sight in his seersucker suit and white panama hat—like some huge grandfather with a ballooning gut. He had dogs—two snarling Rottweilers.

He waved at me and diamonds flashed from rings on his big fingers. Then he smiled, bunching up his red cheeks and pushing his sunglasses far up his long face. It wasn't a friendly smile. When I started to run the dogs snapped their leashes, leaving him with two dangling straps. In a panic, I switched directions and stumbled down toward the edge of that two-hundred-foot drop. The dogs followed, barking, their jaws wet with drool. I was lunch.

Below me was a narrow ledge that snaked along the cliff and disappeared behind the waterfall. That was my only escape—it was that or the snapping teeth of those Rottweilers.

The greasy stranger looked like he was shouting as I lowered myself down onto the ledge. I was shouting too, but nobody could hear anything over the crashing waterfall. The cliff was cold and spray soaked my clothes.

I inched forward.

The dogs kept coming. Their heads were low and mean.

That ledge was slippery as a sheet of ice, but I was going on no matter what. The stranger kept shouting at me as the men shuffled down the ridge. The one with the tattoos raised his crossbow and fired. I flinched, but the arrow broke on the wall between me and the dogs. I inched farther out.

One dog gave up and backed away. One dog stayed and snapped at my feet.

Bang! A chip of rock exploded to my left.

Old Grandpa lowered the rifle from his eye and reloaded—he was shooting at me! How could he? Why would he?

"GRRRR." The second dog closed in, his claws scraping on the tiny ledge, his legs shaky from the strain.

I was at the edge of the falls now, drenched in sweat and spray. The ledge widened out up ahead. If I could make it there, I'd be safe. For a while.

PPOPP! Another shot from the rifle.

One more foot and I would be behind the falls, almost safe. Then the dog snagged my shoelace and pulled. I fell down and banged my chin on the ledge.

The dog didn't make it. I tried to grab him, which was stupid, but he went zooming through the mist, the end of my shoe string still clamped in his jaw.

Scrambling up onto the ledge, I collapsed behind the waterfall. The noise was overpowering. I crawled to the back of the wet little cave and huddled in the semidarkness, shivering. It was a rotten situation, but somehow I didn't feel altogether bad.

All my life I'd waited for some kind of adventure, but I worried that if it ever came I'd probably pass out, not being tough enough. Now men were trying to kill me and I was still alive. I didn't faint. I didn't beg for mercy. I didn't throw up. They had me cornered, but I wasn't backing down.

They were coming into the cave now—I saw the rifle barrel sticking out. I groped on the floor for a rock to throw, but there were none, so I slid backward on my stomach. A hand reached inside the cave. I slipped around a bend just as the stranger's greasy head came into view.

My feet had found an opening in the wall behind me. A wind howled out of the opening, smelling dank and ancient.

"BOY!" The stranger called for me over the crash of the waterfall. Like I was going to come to him. Yeah, sure. Dank or not, I was going through that hole. Suddenly I was in complete and total darkness. The wind was screaming now, probably blowing up from some crevice in the floor behind me.

And then I had a horrible thought.

Spiders.

Hairy spiders. They were probably in here with me. It was a perfect spot for them; they'd love it. For all I knew they were covering the walls, dangling from the ceiling by the millions.

Whatever you do, don't think about spiders, I told myself. Remove them from your mind, or you'll freak out and then the men will kill you. Think about stuff you like. Think about—

"AHH-AAAAHHHHH," I screamed.

Something was in there with me, something lumpy and wet slumped against the wall. It felt exactly like what I thought a dead person would feel, a dead person killed by spiders.

I jumped and started slipping backward. The cave floor was slimy with fungus, my sneakers squealing like baby pigs as I tried to find a foothold. The only thing to grab was the lumpy thing that scared me to begin with.

I grabbed it anyway.

The thing pulled away from the wall with one tug, and came sliding toward my face.

Just my luck. I finally meet a nice girl and the same day I go falling into the center of the earth.

Like grave robbers, the men clambered inside the cavern, their flashlights casting eerie, foggy beams. They'd found me.

"You're a little late!" I hollered up at them as I slid faster and faster and began to fall. I grabbed the lumpy thing and hugged it, pressing it to my face as a shield. Blinded, I waited to hit bottom, only one thought spinning like a mouse on a wheel—How much will it hurt?

CHAPTER *13*

T*hudd!*

I hit some kind of ledge. It was small but big enough for me and the lumpy thing. I was so shaken up I didn't think to check myself for broken bones, which sometimes you don't feel at first if it's cold or you're in shock—I read that somewhere—but nothing hurt. I had banged my knees a little and I was freezing cold. That was it.

The lumpy thing, as it turned out, was a backpack. One of those big internal frame ones they use for climbing Mt. Everest. I felt along its surface for any zippered compartments. There was some strange thing hanging off the top strap. It was heavy and rubbery, maybe a tool or a radio, but I couldn't tell. I couldn't see —I needed a flashlight or matches, anything. The darkness was creeping me out.

I found a flashlight in a side pocket and kissed it before turning it on. "Please work. Please . . ." I said.

Click.

"Oh no . . . "

I was on a ledge that stuck out from a rock wall that was as tall and flat and slick as a glass building. High above me were menacing cracks and wrinkled ridges of lava stone. That stuff could cut like broken bottles. I could never climb out, not even with a ladder.

Down below was a river, hammering underground through a tunnel in the rock and racing who knows where. Everything was huge and dark. Black shadows. Mist. Very creepy.

Then I felt it.

It was so cold that my body was numb and I hadn't felt the tickling until now. I shined the flashlight, squinting to see. Something was covering my legs like a moving blanket. Then I realized what it was. Thousands of green spiders had squirmed out of the pack and over my body, swarming over my feet, marching into my shorts, up my chest. There were hoards of them covering the pack in one sick ocean of hairy legs and twinkling eyes.

But worst of all was how they rushed up to the top of the backpack to swarm over the strange rubbery thing: a human hand, chopped off at the wrist and still gripping the strap on top of the pack.

The whole thing was too much for me. I screamed and started jumping and shaking and trying to brush the spiders off me, but there were too many of them. I kicked at the backpack, got my foot caught in a strap, and tumbled forward, sailing headfirst in a cloud of emerald spiders down into the freezing river.

Swirling and coughing in the frothy water I saw the flashlight! It was sinking! Somehow I dove and caught it—hopefully it was waterproof, even if I wasn't—as water shot up my nose, into my lungs. It took all I had to stay afloat with that rotten pack still wrapped around my ankle and a flashlight gripped in one hand.

The river moved fast, pushing me beneath overhanging rocks, the walls getting closer, the water shooting down a tighter and tighter passage. Suddenly the tunnel became round and steep. Other holes slid by—tunnels splintering off in different directions—and the water was becoming shallower. I was lying on my back, the smooth floor racing under me as the tunnel dipped and curved, sometimes dropping almost straight down. It felt like I was going ninety miles an hour. Everything was spinning and twisting, my shouts clanging against the black, roaring walls. There was nothing to hold on to, no way to stop.

Then in the light of the waterlogged flashlight beam I saw that the tunnel was coming to an end as the river poured down a hole in the floor and disappeared.

I clawed at the walls, but it was no use. The hole swallowed me. I toppled head over heels, the flashlight spinning like a top and flashing every which way—khu-splashh!!!—I hit still water.

Light poured into the grotto—daylight! safety!

Bruised, and bitten all over by spiders, I paddled through a curtain of vines and found myself outside, in a beautiful jungle pool. There were birds and flowers. There was a girl lying in the sun, getting a tan, wearing a bikini so small its purpose was hard to imagine.

The girl was Kate Pierce.

I must be dead, I thought.

Then I passed out.

CHAPTER *14*

When *I came to*, Kate Pierce was giving me mouth-to-mouth resuscitation. I waited awhile before showing signs of consciousness, but soon I felt kind of guilty and opened my eyes. Her hair was hanging in my face.

"Hi," I said.

She sat back and pushed her hair behind her ears, pulled the beach towel tight around her. She looked very serious.

"You look horrendous. Are you okay?" she asked.

"Yeah, thanks," I said.

"What's going on, if you don't mind my asking."

"I don't have a clue. Honestly," I said.

"Don't play games with me, or I'll throw you back in the water. I'm not kidding."

She wasn't kidding.

"Believe me I know this is serious," I said. "Someone's been trying to kill me."

She waited while I sat up slowly and rubbed my eyes. I was trembling and my nose was bleeding some.

"I'm really glad to see you," I said, hoping to lighten up her mood.

"Me too. Now what's going on? Who's trying to kill you?"

"I don't know," I told her. "Some guy. Some guy on the tour. He came late—your father didn't like the looks of him from the beginning. The guy was strange and your dad thought he was a spy. I guess he was, and I shoulda known too, the way he was so weird and laughing at Mr. Norman like that. Then, well, then I saw him out in the woods—I went to take a walk—and he blew up the Zodiac."

"Wait, you're going too fast," said Kate. "What do you mean 'blew up the Zodiac'?!"

"I mean blew it up, as in blow up, as in explosion. Nobody was in the Zodiac. Everyone's fine, don't worry—except for almost me because then they tried to—to kill me, other guys, with dogs and guns."

Kate put her hands on my shoulders to calm me down. I was pretty worked up, I guess, my words stuttering out of my shuddering jaw.

"It's okay," she said. "Just breathe. That's it. Relax. Now please just tell me—slowly—everything that happened."

I did my best. She had to keep slowing me down, asking questions when she didn't understand. I found the story a little hard to buy myself.

When I finished, she just stared at me.

"What's the matter?" I said.

"Water tunnels?" she said. "Rottweilers?"

"There's passageways through the inside of that mountain. Tubes. They go on for miles. I slid all the way down here. That's how I got away from those guys. I nearly died."

She said nothing.

"You never heard of these tubes before?" I said.

"Arron, nobody has. I never have and I know more about this area than maybe anybody. Not counting Dr. Gomasio."

"Well, trust me, they're there," I said.

"Who's pack?" she asked. She was pointing to the soggy backpack lying a few feet away on the shore.

"Don't go near it. I found it inside the mountain. It's filled with spiders."

"What's that on the top? . . . Is that a—!"

"Uh huh." I said, trying hard to sound nonchalant. "It's a hand. I don't know who that belongs to either."

She shuddered and had trouble taking her eyes off the thing.

"Are you okay to walk?" she asked.

"I guess so. How far?"

"A few miles. We've got to move fast to get back to town and radio for help, if Dad's not already back by now. I could leave you here to rest and come back to get you, but I don't know how long that would take and it's probably not so safe for you out here anyway."

"Then I guess I better come with you," I said.

We were about to leave. In a reckless fit of chivalry I had promised to carry the backpack, but now I could hardly bear to look at it. Why did it have to be spiders?

"Are you okay? You look a little pale," Kate said.

"No, I'm fine," I said, disgusted to the core by the very idea of carrying that thing on my back.

"Do you want me to carry it?" she asked.

"Oh no. No . . . I can manage it," I said, still not making a move to pick it up.

"What's wrong?" She was getting impatient. "Is it the hand? I've got a knife, I'll cut it off and we can stuff it inside so it won't bother you."

"I can do that," I said. "Just, would you please do me a favor?"

"Sure."

"Just check it for me. The pack, I mean. To see if it's, uh . . . clean."

"Clean? It's filthy."

"No. I mean . . . check it. For spiders."

"You're afraid of spiders?" she said, beginning to laugh.

"No! I just don't like 'em. I prefer them at a distance."

I was shook up, and now she must think I was the original wimp, the one with his picture in the dictionary under the word *loser*.

"Don't be embarrassed," she said, kindly.

"I'm not."

"Really. It's cute that you're terrified of spiders."

"I'm not terrified," I said weakly.

"It's okay. I'll check for spiders if you take care of that hand."

"It's a deal."

Almost all the spiders had been washed off in the water and what stragglers were left, Kate bravely brushed away. That left me with the hand, which was no picnic. It was still gripping tightly to the nylon strap, so I used Kate's Swiss army knife to cut the strap and gingerly drop the hand into a zippered compartment. Fortunately I didn't have to actually touch it.

Chapter *15*

A*fter a ten-minute hike* we arrived at the trailhead. I was exhausted and winded. Kate helped me out of the pack and chucked it in the back of her decrepit Toyota truck. I climbed in painfully while she coaxed the engine to start.

We sped down Route 56, whipping over the

hairpin turns and little one-lane bridges and roaring onto the dirt road that led to Tunnels Beach.

The gang was all there. I was greeted warmly by everyone except the Normans, who were in a lousy mood and let us all know it.

"I've never been so badly treated in my entire life," said Mr. Norman.

"You people really shouldn't be allowed to take passengers out on the water," said Mrs. Norman

"I want my money back," said Mr. Norman, as he put his wife and son into the taxi they had called. "And you'll be hearing from me if I don't get it. You can count on that."

After the Normans drove away, there was a lot of hugging and carrying on and I even saw a tear from Captain Dan, who quickly brushed it away. They'd been waiting on the beach for the Coast Guard so Dan could file a report.

Everyone wanted to know my story. The general idea had been that I was a goner. Terry had tried to find me after they heard the gunshots, but he hadn't seen anything except bullet shells and footprints. Captain Dan was ready to call in the Park Rangers to go and find me, or what was left of me, and then he was going to notify my parents. That would have been bad. Explaining this afternoon to my mother just wouldn't have been possible.

Everyone was talking at once, asking me

questions about what I'd seen, who blew up the boat, and what happened to the stranger.

Kate hushed them all down. "Give him some room, guys. He's had a tough afternoon. You'll all hear what happened later."

Then she dragged me and Captain Dan over to her truck for a private meeting. She wanted him to hear it first, before the others found out and blabbed the story all over the island.

I told the captain about seeing the creepy guy blow up the Zodiac, about the walkie-talkie, about the booby trap, the shoot out, the other guys, and the dogs. When I got to the part about me climbing along the cliff, Kate said, "Are you ready for this, Dad? This is big stuff. Don't forget anything, Arron. It's important to remember every detail."

I told him about the cave behind the waterfall, the connecting chambers, and how I fell into the bowels of the earth. And about the backpack, the spiders, and the hand.

"A human hand?" blurted Captain Dan.

"Just wait," said Kate.

I continued, telling about the fall into the river and the slide all the way down to the grotto. Then Kate excitedly broke in and finished the story.

For a long moment Captain Dan just held his hairy chin and looked into the distance.

"Is that the pack?" he asked, nodding at the thing in the back of the truck.

"Show him," said Kate.

I unzipped the pocket on the outside of the pack and dumped out the hand. Now I found it totally disgusting and it made me a little sick. Dan stared at it.

"Ordinarily, I wouldn't believe a damn word of this, Mr. Pendleton," said Captain Dan, staring me over with beady eyes. "But my daughter believes you, and she's never wrong about people. Never."

"It's all true, sir, every single word," I said.

"Do you have any idea how important these tunnels could be?" he asked pointing at my nose. "You're a walking miracle, kid. You could be bigger than Captain Cook. Than Columbus."

"I really didn't do anything," I said. "It was all an accident."

"Don't matter. I mean, if I were you, I wouldn't admit that. But it really doesn't make any difference. Anyway, for the time being we've all got to keep totally quiet about this until I do some thinking. The Coast Guard will investigate, file some standard report about my boat. But don't say a word to anyone about the rest of this business. I'll go through the backpack tonight, see if it tells us anything. That okay with you?"

I nodded. I thought the police should know my story, but then my parents would hear all about it too, and I wanted to avoid that. They tend to worry.

"Okay with both of you?"

Kate nodded too.

"All right," he continued. "I've got some ideas already. How about I take you to dinner later? It's the least I can do after all the trouble you've had today. We can have a powwow."

"Thanks, but I should really get back to my parents tonight. They're expecting me."

"How about tomorrow? In the morning," he said.

"He was coming by the store anyway, weren't you Arron?" asked Kate. She remembered! She remembered!!

"Fine," said the captain. "See you tomorrow, then."

He assessed me for a moment, nodding slowly. "Are you okay?" he asked.

"I feel a little nauseous, to tell you the truth."

"It's to be expected," he said. "Kate will give you a ride back to town. I've gotta go file this report and make everyone happy. What a day. Jeepers, I can't believe what they did to my boat. Anyhow, see you in the morning." He patted me on the shoulder, kissed Kate good-bye, and muttered, "Cutest darn couple I ever saw."

Then he smiled mischievously and lumbered back to the beach, leaving us alone, digging our toes in the sand like bashful six-year-olds.

CHAPTER *16*

"Look at this, would you?" mumbled my father, grappling with the morning paper, a spoon, and half a papaya, which spun in its dish of ice like it didn't want to be eaten. He held up the front page of the *McKraft Examiner* and pointed to the bottom blurb. There was mention of an exploded Zodiac, with a picture of the rubbery carnage.

No one at the breakfast table so much as looked up; they were all engrossed in their own reading. Tracy colored dinosaurs, her tongue slipping through her missing front teeth so it almost touched her nose.

"Sweetheart, look," said my father, so my mother had to look at the front page. She studied the photograph.

"My goodness," she said. "Thank heavens you weren't on that boat, Arron. You will be careful today, won't you? We don't know these people, you know . . ."

"Mom, please," I said. "I've got a job at a deli. What could possibly happen?"

"They have knives at delis. Besides, I can't understand why you'd want to work at a deli on your vacation."

"Mom."

"Sweetheart, let the boy alone."

"The people are great. You would love them, Mom, really. I've got to go or I'll be late."

I got up and kissed my parents good-bye.

"There must be a girl," said Lisa. "I mean, I'm sitting here thinking, 'Why is my little brother so anxious to go to work at a deli,' and I realized. A girl. It has to be."

"It doesn't have to be anything, Lisa."

"I think it is, that's all I'm going to say," she said with her nose way up in the air and at the same time buried deep into *Elle* magazine.

"Good-bye, Arron," said my mom. "Don't be late. I'm still glad that wasn't your boat that got blown up."

"It was my boat."

"Funny," said my father. "Very funny."

"Our son the comedian. Don't say such things," called my mother as I wended my way through the tables of buffet-crazed tourists.

I took the eleven-o'clock shuttle bus and was walking into Dan's office by three minutes after twelve. The place was buzzing with excitement.

The gang was clustered over the remains of the exploded Zodiac. They had dumped the wreck on the floor of the hangar and were poking around its slashed carcass, looking for clues. It was wet and gross, like a huge dead sea monster.

Kate came over to kiss me hello and all of a sudden I felt shy, like the first time I met her.

Maybe because she looked so pretty, I don't know, but I felt kind of dopey standing there, shifting my weight from side to side and taking my hands in and out of my pockets. She didn't seem to notice, anyway.

I said hi to Joanne and Craig, then Dan introduced me to Sammy and Vance Viebermann. Sammy was this great old friend of Dan's, pure-blooded Hawaiian and very cool. He had a limp and a scar across his nose that would have killed a lesser man. Vance, on the other hand, was big and blond and perfect and told everybody about what a great athlete he was. I couldn't stand the sight of him.

"Where's Terry?" I asked.

Captain Dan pointed up at the loft where Terry's leg hung over the side of the bed.

"He's letting the alcohol evaporate," said Captain Dan. "He was a bad boy last night. Last I saw, his eyes looked like two cherry jaw breakers. Craig, go see if he's still alive, will you?"

"He got drunk?" I asked.

"He sure did," said Kate. "I practically had to carry him home. I think he blabbed about what happened yesterday."

"You *think*?" said Dan. "He was standing on the bar screaming at the top of his lungs. The whole island knows by now."

He got me a soda and brought me and Kate

back to a worktable under the loft. It was cleared off and the backpack's contents were spilled out. There were notebooks, maps, tools, some freeze-dried goulash, and several collecting jars containing insects and dried rodent skulls. Everything had been sealed in plastic, so the water hadn't destroyed it.

Dan held up a copy of the *McKraft Examiner* and showed me the headline: "Worst Feared for Missing Student," it read.

"Been following this story?" Captain Dan asked.

"Saw something about it the other day," I said. "Is this what you came up with? If it's already in the paper, Captain, I think they're a little ahead of you."

Dan read from the article:

"For five days now, authorities have been alerted to the disappearance of Alistair Courtenay Vaneblone III, twenty-seven, a student from England's Bulwer Science Academy. In Kauai on a research grant, Mr. Vaneblone had been attempting to complete his thesis on ancient Polynesian culture. He was last seen at Hanalei's Ching Yung Shopping Village where he was apparently purchasing supplies for his final week of roughing it in Kokee State Park. Mr. Vaneblone . . ."

"Ahhh, blah blah blah. You get the picture anyway."

I nodded my head. "So what's the connection?"

Captain Dan handed me one of the journals from the pile. I opened it and read the front page. Printed in flowing script was the name Alistair Courtenay Vaneblone III.

"Gee whiz," I said. "Was that his hand?"

Captain Dan nodded.

"How do you know?"

"It was wearing a Bulwer Science Academy class ring."

"So he's dead . . ." I was feeling a little weak in the knees. "Are you saying—?"

"That he was murdered? Yes," said Captain Dan. "How his hand was still hanging on the back of his luggage, I don't know. Pretty spooky. I s'pose the rest of him is down in those tunnels you found, but as for why, my theory is Vaneblone just knew too darn much. He was probably on to something very big, a major discovery. I haven't read all his journals and maps yet, but I did look them over. There's some pretty wild things in there; most of it is downright nuts. I think he may have been a bit granola up in the brain and I wouldn't buy any of it if it weren't for one simple thing."

"What?" I asked.

"The tunnel you found. He wrote about it. He'd been there too, though I don't think he got as far down as you did. But your descriptions of the caves and the chambers behind the waterfall are the same as his. According to Vaneblone, that's just the beginning of many."

"But why would anybody want to kill him for that?" I asked.

"Any number of reasons," said Kate.

"Maybe competitors. Maybe they tried to steal these books. Maybe Vaneblone was snooping around and found somebody's stash of drugs," said Captain Dan.

"Drugs?" I asked.

"Could be. All kinds of weird stuff goes on in those hills."

"Do you think the people who blew up your boat and tried to kill me are the same people who killed Vaneblone?" I asked.

"Smart kid."

"I told you, Dad," said Kate. "You see, Arron? If you take this one more step, what do you maybe have?"

"I don't know . . . Stingray Cruises? You think so? But this is all crazy. Captain, this is crazy. Why . . . why would . . . "

"It's always money, my boy," said Captain Dan. "Somebody stands to make a lot of it, or lose a lot of it, or they wouldn't go through all the trouble.

Money," he said again, dreamily. "Buried treasure maybe. Hehehe." He laughed. "Hmmmm . . ." he growled.

"So, what are you going to do now?" I asked.

"You found the tunnels, you found the backpack. What do you think?"

"Gosh," I said. "I don't know anything about this stuff. Have you called the police?"

"No!" said Captain Dan.

"No?"

"Not yet," said Kate.

"Are you planning to?"

"No way!" said Captain Dan.

"But we have to," I said. "We suspect a crime, a murder. We're supposed to notify the authorities, aren't we?"

"By law, yes," said Captain Dan. "But authorities aren't always authorities, if you get my drift."

"But we have his hand. We can't just keep it."

"Sure we can. It's in formaldehyde with my exotic fish. Nobody will know."

We went down the street to the Shell House for lunch: Kate, Captain Dan, Craig, and I. Over sandwiches Dan said that he wanted to see this cave for himself. He would go with the whole crew very early the next morning and he asked if I wanted to come, promising it would be safe since all the guys would be there. Of course he needed me to go, in order to find the waterfall and the cave, but he never let on to that.

I looked toward Kate. "Are you going?"

She nodded.

"I'll go," I said.

"Well, aren't we the eager young lad all of a sudden?" said Captain Dan. He and Craig shared a knowing glance and Craig said, "Ooohh," around a mouthful of hamburger. Kate blushed, then hauled off and punched him in the arm so hard he winced.

"Grow up, guys," she said.

The captain was about to pay the check when an enormous Hawaiian woman entered the Shell House followed by a small entourage of people. She was about sixty and walked with a cane, shifting her three hundred or so pounds almost gracefully. She wore a blue muumuu and had her black hair done up with a red flower behind her ear. The smoke from her cigar flowed around her like a veil. Everyone in the restaurant hushed when she entered. I couldn't tell if it was from fear or respect.

Captain Dan got up and embraced the old woman. "Mama! It's so good to see you! How are you feeling?"

She hugged him casually. "Oh, doing mo' better Daniel. What be up with you?"

"I've got someone I want you to meet," said Dan. "Can you sit with us for a moment?"

The woman waved her group away and they sat

down at a table across the room. Dan seated the woman carefully, then sat down next to her. She was right across from me but did not deign to acknowledge anyone's existence till Kate and Craig said a formal "Good afternoon, Mama Kauai." It was like a ritual; afterward she warmed up.

"Mama, I want you to meet our new friend, Arron Pendleton," said the captain.

Her old eyes surveyed me. "This the boy that everyone been talkin' about?" she asked.

"You heard about it then?" asked Captain Dan.

"Hmmm. Mama Kauai hear everything that happen on her island, you know that. Mama Kauai hear things that happen way long before they happen. You understand that, don't you child?" she asked Kate.

"Yes, Mama Kauai. Thank you," she replied.

"Yes," continued the old woman. "I hear this boy, he go an' find something maybe better he don't find."

"Mama, it was an accident. I didn't mean any harm," I said.

"Don't worry yourself about it, child. It can't be helped. Anyhow, Mama Kauai don't believe in any accidents. There is no such thing. It all come down for a good reason."

There was a pause and I heard some thunder roll around in the hills. It seemed to get a little darker in the Shell House.

"Just you be careful, son. The Menehune are out there and they don't want to be disturbed. You want them friendly with you, not mad. Menehune are powerful spirits, let me tell you. They can make a lot of big trouble. Better you not get involved in that kind of magic, hmmm? Understand?"

"I'm sorry, but I don't know what that is—Menehune." I stammered.

"Little people," said Captain Dan, with a nervous laugh. "Like elves. It's an old wives' tale, you know. Nothing to worry about, right, Mama?"

Mama Kauai looked at him coldly. "Mama Kauai says what she means. It's no legend, Daniel Pierce, you best remember that. And you got no right dragging this boy into it. You of all people should know to listen to old Mama Kauai."

With that she got up and sauntered, almost sassily, over to her table, leaving us in a mild state of shock. Craig whistled the theme to *The Twilight Zone* under his breath.

"Who the heck was she?" I whispered.

"She," said Captain Dan, "is the one and only Mama Kauai. Self-declared First and Only Lady of the island. She owns the Mama Kauai Bar and Grill next door. I love her, but I got to admit, she's a little soft in the head."

"She is not, Dad," said Kate, sounding pretty defensive. It was obvious she liked the woman. "She's pure Hawaiian, she's proud, and I love her. Mom loved her too."

There was a brief silence.

"She's a little scary," I said.

"She isn't," said Kate. "Not if you know her. She's just . . . old-fashioned. She believes in the old ways."

"She is a little odd, Kate," said Craig. "But she does give the best luau on the island, I'll say that for her."

"What was she talking about?" I asked. "Was she serious about me staying out of this? And what are those things, those Menehune? Are they real? No one told me about any elves."

"Relax," said Captain Dan. "It's a legend, an old wives' tale. The Menehune were supposedly a race of little people here on Kauai before the Polynesian settlers. Like Pygmies, or something."

"More like trolls," said Craig.

"Okay, like trolls. Whatever. Nobody really knows. Anyway, legend says that when the Polynesians arrived on Kauai from Tahiti and Samoa, the Menehune went to live inside caves, only to come out at night. They were very private little fellas and didn't appreciate the new guys on the block. And, as the legend goes, they do stuff for you if you give them food."

"And say a chant very nicely," said Kate.

"Right," continued the captain. "They can build fences or plant fields, stuff like that. They can do bad stuff too. They're supposed to be magic. Anyway, that's the story and it's just a story. No one's ever seen them."

"That's not true and you know it, Dad," said Kate. "Lots of people see strange things on this island. They swear they have."

"I saw something once, but I think it was a wild pig," said Craig.

"Fine," said Captain Dan. "What I mean is, no normal person has ever seen one. Mama Kauai doesn't count; she sees stuff that's not there all the time. Of course, sometimes she's right." He chuckled.

We left the Shell House and walked quietly back toward the hangar. I had a lot to think about.

"I don't think I'm cut out for this, guys," I said.

"What do you mean?" Kate asked.

"I mean, I'm from New York. I'm out of my element with all this. Look, first I'm nearly murdered running away from bad guys, and then this whole thing with this Vaneblone guy's severed hand. And now trolls . . . and you want me to go back in there tomorrow?! I really don't know. I think you should handle this."

There was a long silence.

Finally Captain Dan said, "If you chicken out of this I'll forbid you to see my daughter ever again."

I laughed, but when I looked at Kate's face, I could tell he wasn't joking.

Chapter 17

"So, what's New York like?" asked Kate.

We were walking with Spartacus back to the deli, and it was hard to imagine there ever was such a place as New York.

"It's a mess," I said. "It's just like this, except without the trees and mountains and flowers, and the people are mean. And the animals mostly carry diseases and you can't touch them."

"Sounds wonderful," she said.

"But there are some good things too. We've got some of the finest acid rain and smog this side of Mexico City. Traffic all hours of the day, noise, water pollution. I think we hold some kind of record for poisoned shellfish."

She laughed. "I want to go anyway."

"You're crazy. Why would you want to leave this? Even for a second?"

"Because I never have," she said. "I've been to Maui a couple times and to Honolulu once, but I was a baby. I want to travel. I want to go to the ballet and the opera . . . and I want to go to a big college in a big city and learn something important, something . . . I don't know . . . "

"Like what?"

"Like dance, and art, and what the world is like outside this little rock in the middle of the Pacific

Ocean. I mean, it's a great rock, as rocks go, but I want something more."

"Well," I said, "you'll go. And I'm sure you'll go to a great college, if that's what you want."

All she did was give a quick laugh as she shook her head and kept on walking.

We came to the little Tropical Deli and found Dr. Gomasio putting away his fish and polishing up his knives like he was packing up for the day. He waved a meat cleaver at us and shouted, "Hello!" To me he said, "Ahh! The New York Boy comes back. Good to see you. You too, Kate san."

"What are you doing, Doc? It's not even one thirty."

"I'm closing up early. Too much going on, there's too much shooting and blowing up boats. You're lucky nobody got killed. I'm going home and meditate. You look after the New York Boy, but it's not so safe in the deli now. I'll open in a day or so, okay?"

"Okay, if you say so," said Kate.

"Hei, I so say," Doc said. Then he pointed to me and motioned to the other side of the room. "You— go over there."

"What? Where?" I asked.

"Over by Kate. Go on."

I went and stood where he wanted.

"What are you going to do?" asked Kate.

82

"Give him a test."

"A test? But Doc—"

"Shh, Kate san. You ready, boy?"

"I don't know," I said. "What are you gonna do?"

He didn't answer, just stood there at the counter about ten feet away. Then, without any warning, he picked up three eggs and threw them at me, one right after the other.

"What?!" I yelped, but decided I better concentrate on catching the eggs which were all three sailing through the air right toward me. The first one was easy—I caught it gently in my right hand. The second was also a cinch, I caught that in my left. But the third was a problem. I didn't have time to put egg number 1 in my left hand in order to free my right, and I didn't have the brains just to hold on to eggs numbers 1 and 2, letting egg number 3 drop and do what eggs do. Instead I dropped eggs 1 and 2, caught egg 3 with my two hands and promptly smashed it.

Kate cracked up laughing.

"Pretty good," said Doc.

"What the hell did you do that for?" I said, slimy strings of yolk dripping off my fingers.

"It was a test," he said.

I washed my hands and Kate cleaned the mess off the floor. Doctor Gomasio went back to work, chuckling to himself.

"What kind of a test? . . . A test for what?" I was completely confused.

"Doc, next time don't use the organic eggs," said Kate. "They're too expensive."

"So are you going to tell me what that all meant?" I asked. "Did I pass the test at least?"

"I'm not going to say. Think about it," was his answer.

Soon Doc said good-bye and went home, with a warning that we both be careful. "Watch your step," he said. "One person dead is plenty enough."

Kate and I stayed to clean and lock up the deli. By the time we finished I had this idea to invite her back to the hotel for dinner. As she shut the door and locked it, I managed to work up the courage to ask her. She looked nervous for a second.

"I, I uh, I don't know. I really . . . My dad may need my help with stuff to get ready for tomorrow."

"Okay, well, if he says it's all right, how about it?"

"I'm not . . . ummm. It's just . . . ." she said.

My heart sank.

"Well, whatever. It's just that I've got to spend some time with my parents or they'll worry about me, and I thought, you know, you might want to come too. That is if you want to."

My heart was pounding and she was staring at the bandanna she twisted in her hands. What was it, I thought? Did she hate me? Did I do something wrong, cross some line? Some Hawaiian no-no?

"I have to tell my dad but, sure," she said, "I'd love to go."

I started to breathe again.

Chapter 18

Craig *was using the pickup* so we had to shuttle-bus over to the hotel. That was fine, since it gave us time to talk and for Kate to play tour lady, pointing out all the important sites along the way.

It was a fast hour, and before I knew it the doors opened and we stepped out next to the fake volcano, which was broken. Filthy workmen crawled around underneath the plastic mountain adjusting pipes and valves. Others stood motion-less in the fountain with disgusted looks on their faces.

Kate wrinkled up her nose at the volcano and then, as we entered the lobby, she stopped in her tracks and scowled fiercely at everything else she saw.

"Pretty gaudy, ain't it?" I said. "Who the heck would've dreamed up a thing like this?"

"Lewis B. McKraft is who," said Kate, staring up at the hugeness of the place.

"Who?"

"L. B. McKraft. It's his hotel. He owns most of the big hotels on Kauai, or at least most of the stock. This is his newest. God, I haven't been inside here since they started it. They keep getting worse and worse."

"A tad overdone, I admit."

"It's disgusting," she said with emphasis on the gust part. "He could single-handedly destroy the whole island." She looked mad enough to blow the place up.

"Do you want to go? I mean, we can if it offends you."

"No way. It's still early; let's go swimming," she said. "And I don't know about you, but I'm starving—of course I'm always hungry . . . "

Truthfully, I'm always hungry too and I never needed to be asked twice when food was concerned. So I just said, "Follow me then," and raced down to the beach. We stayed there for hours, eating, swimming, boogie-boarding and snorkeling till it got kind of late and the sun started to set bright red over the island of Niihau.

I had absolutely the greatest time. Kate and I were like old friends. Despite that I had a crush on her and not knowing at all how she felt about me, I was relaxed—it wasn't like spending time with A GIRL. It was like spending time alone, only much, much better.

"So you brought a girl over for dinner, eh?"

I was in the lobby talking to my dad on the house phone, trying to find out what time to meet them. He wasn't making it easy. They always razz me about girls I like and it drives me crazy, but it was my fault for leaving them a message at the desk about bringing "a friend."

"Yeah, but it's no big deal. Don't make a whole big thing about it."

"I'm not making a big thing. Did I say anything?" asked my dad.

"No. But I know how your mind works."

"I'm glad for you," he said. "Needless to say, your mother was thrilled to read your message."

"I'll bet she was."

"So, what's she like?"

"She's standing here, Dad, next to me."

"What? What does she look like?"

"Father—"

"Oh," he said. "I see. Well, I guess you can't really go into detail, then. Not with her right there."

"That's right, Dad."

"But you could just answer yes or no to my questions."

"Dad—"

"Gorgeous?"

"Yes. Dad—"

"Blonde?"

"Brown—Dad!"

He was laughing. "Meet us at the restaurant in a half hour."

It took a three-dollar bribe for Robby to watch *Heckle and Jekyll* in my parents' suite while Kate and I took turns going up to shower and change. Kate went first while I browsed through magazines at the gift shop. She came down in fifteen minutes looking pretty amazing in pleated slacks and a white shirt fastened at the neck with a silver clasp—stuff she'd thrown in her pack before we left Hanalei. I never expected her to be so stylish. For days all I'd seen were shorts and T-shirts.

"Your closet was open," she said, braiding her wet hair as she came off the elevator. "That blue tie is beautiful."

I was back down in ten minutes wearing the blue tie and probably too much after-shave, though you can never be too sure. We hurried to the restaurant down an endless trail of covered walkways lit by bamboo torches. The flames sputtered in the wind and big drops of rain began to patter on the leaves.

"I'm nervous," said Kate.

"There's nothing to be nervous about." Then I thought of introducing Kate to my parents and Lisa, with her sarcastic, mocking glances at me and my DATE. And who only knew what might come out of Robby's mouth. Or Tracy's. I also remembered all the details of my adventures that I couldn't tell them about yet. I felt a cold breeze and yellow lightning flashed far out at sea.

"I'm nervous too," I said.

CHAPTER 19

"So, Katherine . . ." began my mother after we all sat down and got comfortable. It always started off like that—"So, Katherine," or "So tell me, Katherine," or "So, Katherine, tell me"—and it went on and on from there.

My parents love to delve in the minds of innocent bystanders. They talk to almost anybody. Waiters, plumbers, doormen, ballerinas, stenographers (no lawyers), lobster fishermen, political theorists (no politicians), lion tamers, psychologists. They really love psychologists.

"Well, actually, I never went to high school," Kate admitted at one point, "so college is kind of out of the question. Even if my dad could afford to send me."

My mother was shocked, and Lisa, the Princess of Higher Education, raised her eyebrows.

"You're not going to college?" she asked.

"I'd like to, but . . ." Kate shrugged.

"You mean you never went to school at all?" said my mother.

"Elementary school."

"How did you manage that?" asked my father. "They didn't force you to go?"

"No," she said. "I don't know how exactly. I just never went after sixth grade. I remember being tested by a psychologist, or a teacher a long time ago. I shook him up pretty badly."

"Why?" asked my dad.

"My IQ was too high and I kind of knew stuff I shouldn't have known."

"And that scared him?" asked my mom. "Wasn't much of a psychologist, was he?"

"Well," said Kate, "I told him his house was on fire. He didn't believe me, but five minutes later a neighbor called and told him his boiler had exploded. The fire department was just leaving. I guess it shook him up. He ran out of the office and never finished the session."

There was a small but noticeable silence.

"You had psychic abilities as a child?" asked my father.

"I still do . . . sometimes."

"My goodness, that's fascinating," said my mother.

"Hmmm," said my father. "That certainly is fascinating."

"What's sidekick ability?" asked Tracy.

"Psychic," said my mother.

"Okay, psychic," repeated Tracy. "So what is it?"

"It's like Wonder Woman, stupid," said Robby.

Kate laughed and my parents pretended they didn't hear it.

"That's not very nice, Robby," said Lisa.

"Well, it's true," he said.

"No, it's not," I said. "Tracy, psychic ability means ESP. You know what that is?"

Tracy's eyes widened in amazement. "You have ESP?!"

"Tracy, keep your voice down, please," said my mother. "I'm sorry about her, Katherine."

"That's okay," said Kate, laughing. "I don't mind."

"Can you, like, give us a demonstration?" asked Lisa.

"Lisa!" said my mother.

"What?"

"Dad—" I said.

"Please?" Lisa asked. "I've never seen anyone be psychic before."

"Lisa, Kate doesn't want to," I said, but inside I was burning with curiosity.

"It's all right, Arron," said Kate. "I don't mind."

"How does it work?" my father asked, leaning over the table, chin in hand, wild with enthusiasm.

"Well," said Kate, "first of all, everyone's got psychic ability, but most people don't know it. They never have the opportunity to use it."

"I don't have it," said my mother. "I wish I did. I

never know anything that's going on in this world."

"What am I thinking?" asked Robby.

"Can you talk to aliens?" asked Tracy.

"C'mon guys, this isn't a circus," I said, feeling terrible for Kate. She didn't mind at all, though. She looked amused.

"Oh, please, you have to," said Lisa. "Just do something a little bit psychic."

"I don't know . . ." said Kate.

"Don't feel pressured, Katherine," said my father. "But we do have open minds here. Judy and I were at Woodstock. We've seen all kinds of things."

"It would be fascinating, Katherine, but whatever makes you feel comfortable," my mother said.

"Listen guys," I said, getting a little defensive, "she already said she didn't want to, so let's forget it."

"It's okay, Arron," said Kate. "I'll try to do something." She centered herself and became quiet.

"How would you like to go about this?" asked my dad, all six of us hushed with anticipation. "Should I think of a color? a flower? a piece of music? Do you know any songs from the sixties?"

"No, I like jazz," said Kate. "I have an idea—" She called our waiter, Bret, over to the table. Bret was eager and not too bright.

"Have you folks decided on your order?" He spoke words like some people lift weights.

"I would like to order for the gentleman first," said Kate.

Bret looked confused but said nothing.

"May I, Mr. Pendleton?" Kate asked my dad.

"Be my guest," said Dad, not believing she could do it.

Kate began. "The gentleman will have the Caesar salad, onion soup, and whatever fish you recommend to have blackened Cajun style, though my personal advice would be the mahimahi. Right now he'd like a Perrier, but with dinner he'll have a glass of house white wine. He'll want fresh pepper on the salad, but not the soup. And make sure the fish is done pretty well, because he'll send it back if it's too rare.

"I know ordinarily you wait to take dessert orders, but later on he'll want a cup of decaf. And he doesn't know it now, but when you bring the dessert cart over, he's going to ask you for a piece of macadamia mud pie, assuming there's any left. Thank you. I think the rest of us will be a few minutes."

"Very well," Bret said and left.

My father's jaw was scraping along the table top. We all looked at him to see what he was going to say.

"Well?" asked Kate. "Was I close?"

"Amazing," said my dad.

"Well, Dad, was she right?" Lisa asked.

"Down to the letter," he said, unable to believe what just happened. "Will I really order the mud pie?"

"Yes," said Kate. "But you'll regret it later."

All of us at the table gave her a short round of applause as she wiped her brow and took a long drink of water.

Kate predicted something else that evening.

It is a Pendleton tradition for my father to embarrass his children by calling a restaurant beforehand to have the waiters gather 'round our table and sing "Happy Birthday" to us. We never know who the victim will be, or when he'll do it, though we know it won't be on our birthday.

He had planned to surprise me that night, but luckily Kate picked up on it and gave it away. Everyone was very impressed. I thanked her from the bottom of my heart.

All in all, things went well for a while. I was happy to be sitting next to Kate with my family. Once the ESP thing died down, Kate fit in very nicely with everyone. The food started coming and we ate and didn't have a care in the world. It was turning out to be a perfect night in paradise. I started thinking things had never been so lovely, when I looked up and saw something that made me inhale a wad of ono fish and choke.

The big man in the seersucker suit was here,

the one from yesterday, the one with the Rottweilers. He was wearing a white suit now, his hair was combed, and he was with his wife, but I knew instantly it was him.

"Put your arms up in the air, sweetheart," said my mother while Lisa hit me on the back.

"Are you okay? Arron, are you all right?" she asked.

"Fine," I wheezed, trying to get control of myself.

The big man and his wife were being led to their table by the maitre d'. They were going to pass right by our table.

OH GEEEZ, I thought. WHAT DO I DO? WHAT IS HE DOING HERE? HOW COULD THEY LET HIM IN HERE?

He came closer. I knew any second he would spot me. Quickly, I knocked my silverware on the floor.

"Whoops," I said. "I better get that."

I slipped out of my chair and crawled under the table just as the maitre d' stomped past us. I grabbed Kate's leg as the man's size 14 shoes squeaked by. I was suddenly drenched in cold sweat.

"The boy's gone crazy," said my father.

"What do you mean gone crazy," Lisa jibed. "How can he go crazy if he's always been crazy to begin with."

My mother, who did not like scenes, smiled and spoke through her teeth. "Arron, dear, get back up to the table. Let the waiter, or somebody, do that."

Kate lifted up the tablecloth and poked her head down. I shivered in the dark like a mouse in a cobra cage.

"Arron, what is it?" she whispered.

"You have the ESP, you tell me."

"Who do I look like, a magician? What is wrong with you?"

"I have to talk to you," I said. "I'm going to get up and go to the bathroom. Follow me."

"What is it?"

"Please. Do what I say."

I climbed back into my chair and sat like a mannequin, a crooked, fake smile on my face. I glanced over to try and spot my pal. He was seated across the restaurant, far away from me, but close enough to see me just fine if he looked this way.

I knew it. He's come to kill me.

"I-have-to-go-to-the-bathroom-excuse-me," I blurted, then shot out of my seat and darted for the door.

In the men's room I splashed a lot of cold water on my face and stared into the mirror.

This can't be happening, I told myself. It just can't.

Kate met me in the bar and I dragged her out the front door to stand under the awning. It was raining heavily now. The cool breeze calmed me a little.

"Arron, what is it?" she asked, very concerned.

"That big man who just walked in, that older guy in the white suit, did you see him?"

"Yes."

"Kate, he was there the other day when they were shooting at me. He's one of them."

Her look was as grave as could be.

"Arron, are you absolutely positive it's the same man?"

"Yes, absolutely the same guy. Why? Why are you looking at me like that? What is it?"

"Are you sure he was there with those men?"

"Kate," I said, exasperated. "I remember it exactly. He was there. I think he's the boss man."

"Are you certain?"

"Kate! Yes! Why? What is it?"

"Arron, the man who just walked in, the big, tall man in the white suit—he owns this hotel—"

"WHAT?"

"That man is L. B. McKraft."

CHAPTER *20*

Going *back into the restaurant* took most of my guts. Believe me, I didn't want to, but I couldn't very well run out of the hotel without letting my folks know. So Kate and I slipped back to the table and tried to act as if nothing happened. All the while I kept my head cocked to the right, like some moron, so the man in the seersucker suit wouldn't see my face.

The moment dinner was over, I stretched and said it was a shame Kate had to leave so early. She played right along, looking at her watch and saying that it was indeed getting late.

"I was thinking I'd take the shuttle with her to Hanalei," I told my parents. "I mean, I'll come back, but I just want to, you know . . . "

"Escort your date?" said Lisa.

"Keep her company on the ride," I corrected. "I'll be back in a couple hours."

My father agreed wholeheartedly, my mother half so, but only if Hanalei was safe at night. I assured her it was probably safer than the Blue Egret Hotel.

Up in my room, Kate sat on the edge of the bed and watched *Magnum P.I.* while I threw some stuff into my backpack. A couple extra T-shirts, shorts, a bathing suit, a toothbrush—just to be on the safe side. I said I'd be back in two hours, but with things as they were at the hotel, coming back might not be such a good idea. I jammed every-thing in the bag along with all those brochures I'd collected, slung the bag over my shoulder, and stood at the door with a horrible, oozing, molasses-dripping fear in the pit of my stomach. Tom Selleck was shooting at someone from behind a barrel of toxic chemicals.

"My favorite episode," Kate said.

"Uh, don't you think we should leave? Like, immediately?" I said.

"Yes," she said. "But is there another way out of here? A fire escape, or a vine off your balcony, or something?"

"No. It's eight stories straight down—why?"

"Because any second now there's gonna be a knock on your door and I think—"

There was a knock on my door.

"How did you know that?" I whispered, terrified of who it might be.

"Takes kidneys," she said, pointing to her head. "Better answer it if we can't climb down the balcony."

At my door was a big guy wearing a blue blazer and a fake smile. His name tag read TAD.

"Mr. Pendleton?" he said.

"Who wants to know?"

"I'm Tad. Mr. McKraft asked me to give this to you." He handed me a piece of note paper that read:

Mr. Pendleton,

I'm glad I spotted you. Been meaning to have a friendly chat. Why don't we meet in the library. Tad will show you the way. Ask the lovely Miss Pierce—

that is her name isn't it?—to wait for you in the lobby. This, as you understand, is man-to-man business.

Lewis B. McKraft

It wasn't an invitation. It was an "or else," like a kidnapping with good manners. Tad wasn't about to let us out of his sight. There would be no arguing, and definitely no getting away from him, so I shrugged and he led us, without talking, to the library.

This library was tucked away at the far end of the lobby. Its doors were shut and locked. Tad stopped, turned to Kate, and said, "Beat it."

"You just watch it, mister—" said Kate, sounding like her father. "Are you gonna be okay, Arron?"

"You tell me."

"You'll be fine. I'll knock in five minutes to get you."

"Mr. Mckraft said ten minutes," Tad reminded us.

"Tough," said Kate. "I'll knock in five."

She kissed me on the cheek and left us. Tad knocked twice, took out a key, and opened the door. McKraft was sitting in a leather armchair next to a fire, a children's picture book open on his lap. There were bookcases stretching up to the ceiling and a glass cabinet with old photographs and artifacts on display. Some of these were horrible things, grimacing masks and spiky fish leering down from their shelves.

"I'll make sure you're not disturbed, Mr. McKraft."

"Marvelous, Tad, thank you very much," said McKraft in a loud southern accent. Tad shut the door behind me.

"Mr. Pendleton, it is a pleasure." McKraft got up, all six feet four inches of him, and shook my hand. "Please, have a seat. Make yourself at home," he said acting as gracious and kind as anyone could be. "Do you like books?"

"Yeah, sure," I said.

"So do I," he said with great enthusiasm. "I love them. I've read all kinds of books. Great big Russian novels. Science books. Autobiographies. Short stories. But you know, my favorite kind of book is—and you might find this funny—but my favorite kind are children's books. Like this here."

He held up what he was reading. It was a book that I'd loved as a kid, about a little boy who had so many animals he opened his own zoo. That little boy always reminded me of me. I thought about my own animals. Did McKraft know about that? How could he know? How could he know anything about my life, I wondered.

"Children's books ease my mind," McKraft continued. "I find them awfully refreshing. I appreciate their honesty and simplicity. Do you like children's books?"

"When I was a kid," I said.

"I appreciate those same qualities of honesty and simplicity in young people," he said. "That's why I hire a young staff to work with me at my hotels. Tad, for instance, is a very honest, very simple boy. Same qualities I see in you. You seem like a fine young man."

"Thanks," I said, thinking he reminded me both of a general and a used-car salesman.

"I take it you're enjoying our lovely island," he said. "You've made some friends already, even met a charming young lady. That's marvelous. You know, if your parents agree, I'm sure there would be an opening for a young man like yourself at one of my hotels. You do know I own this hotel, don't you?"

"That's what I've heard," I said. "Listen, I don't mean to be rude, but I gotta go. I'm holding people up."

"The girl can wait!" snapped McKraft, suddenly quite serious. "You're right. Let us not pussyfoot around. You know I've got something on my mind. Something I need to get off my chest."

He paused, lit a cigarette, offered me one. I refused.

"What happened between us the other day was a . . . misunderstanding. Simple as that. An incident from . . . from another life, as you young folks say these days. I just wanted you to know one thing. They were shooting at the dogs. They had no intention of harming you, whatsoever."

"I don't know what you're talking about," I said, poker-faced. "You must be thinking of someone else. Nothing happened to me the other day."

"Well put," said McKraft. "Best to forget about it. But before you go—you sure you don't want a cigarette? No? Just as well. Nasty habit—before you go, I wanted to ask you if maybe you've found any interesting things since you've been here. Any artifacts. Anything belonging to someone else. Anything . . . unusual. I have an interest in archeology, as you can see." He pointed to the glass cases.

"Nope," I said.

"Nope, huh?"

"Haven't found much of anything," I said.

"I'm a generous man, Mr. Pendleton. Generous to those I like. If you should come upon anything unusual, information even, give me a call."

"I'll do that."

"You'll be glad you did. Because next time, they won't be shooting at the dogs."

It hadn't even taken five minutes. Kate was sitting patiently in the lobby, looking at her watch. When I walked over, she jumped up and threw her arms around my shoulders.

"I was just going to come get you," she said, hugging me. It sounded like she was starting to cry. I patted her on the back.

"It went okay, Kate. I'm fine," I said. "I'm fine."

"I was scared, Arron."

"Tell me about it," I said. "We better go. Come on, let's get the shuttle."

CHAPTER *21*

Milk *swirled in my coffee* and I watched the steam rise out of the mug, very, very glad to be out of the storm, at Kate's house. She sat with me at her kitchen table. We were both wrapped up in giant bathrobes because our clothes had gotten soaked in the rain and had to be tossed into the dryer.

Captain Dan was in a lousy mood. He paced from room to room, while Joanne stirred a huge pot of chili on the stove. The smell was powerful, drifting through the entire house and making me hungry.

"And the shuttle driver just said the rains were too bad to make it back to the hotel tonight?" The captain was coming back through the kitchen, scratching fiercely at his beard. "Not very professional of him."

"Yeah, I don't think so either," I said, remembering how upset my mother had been on the phone when I told her the same story.

"Hmmmm," said Dan. "But you're sure you saw him—"

"Absolutely. The same driver was sitting in the Busted Schooner, and he was watching every move we made," said Kate.

"Hmmm. Hmmmmmmm," said Dan.

The Busted Schooner was where we finally tracked down Captain Dan and his pirates. Inside, everyone had been loud and rowdy, crowded around a center table to watch Terry and a three-hundred-pound Samoan spearfisherman arm wrestle. I had never seen so much snarling and bulging muscle. Dan stood on a chair to cheer Terry, his right hand clutching a wad of five-dollar bills.

Terry won. His prize was a brown octopus named Reggie who was kept in a barrel by the front door, and when Kate finally hauled her father out to the parking lot, Terry, Craig, and Vance hauled the barrel into the back of Terry's pickup truck. I helped them since they were all too wobbly to even get it through the door without spilling gallons of saltwater all over the sawdust floor. Terrified, Reggie sank to the bottom and suckered on to his barrel for dear life.

Somehow, we all made it back to Dan's house.

"That rotten, stinkin', no-good son-of-a-rat dog . . ." Captain Dan muttered to himself. He scratched and paced and swore at McKraft, saying things I can't begin to repeat.

"Your language, Father!" reprimanded Kate.

"Sorry, sorry . . ." mumbled Dan. "But I can't help it. That bum McKraft doesn't deserve to live! He's a waste of oxygen! I should have known it was him behind all this . . . trying to put me under! Blowing up my boats!"

"They only blew up one boat, Dad," said Kate.

"So?" said Dan. "I only had three to begin with."

"It's a good thing we didn't go to the police," said Kate.

"Why's that?" I asked.

"Because McKraft owns the cops," said Captain Dan. "He buys their cars and guns and uniforms. They would never believe a word we say. It's politics."

Joanne poured us fresh cups of coffee and started to dump a frightening amount of spice into the pot of chili. It bubbled and looked about ready to explode.

"Darn, darn, darn," mumbled the captain, making his thirtieth pass through the kitchen. "I just can't figure this darn thing out. There are too many clues and I can't fit them together, but something tells me they all connect. They have to connect somewhere. But where?"

"Relax, Dan," said Joanne. "You want some chili?"

"No. I'm getting an ulcer as it is. I need a glass of milk."

Joanne got him his milk and he drank it down, wiped his mouth, and belched.

"Father!" said Kate.

"Excuse me," he said. "I'm very agitated."

"You were in a good mood this morning," said Kate. "What happened since then?"

"I went through Vaneblone's diaries, that's what," he said, staring morosely at the table. "I can't make any sense out of them. The boy was crazy . . . he was off his nut. He'd been up in the hills for months before he disappeared, and every week or so he'd come down, muddy and half-crazed, to buy a sandwich and get his mail. He had a post office box in Princeville."

"Well, I read some of those letters. His science academy in England had been trying to track him down to tell him his grant ran out and that he was being kicked out of the university."

"Why?" Kate asked.

"Because he was a kook, that's why. They didn't want anything to do with him. They wanted him out of science altogether. He was living like a crazy person in the jungle. The Park Rangers were after his hide too because his camping permit ran out, but they could never find him. He kept getting away from them."

"And you found nothing in his notes?" Kate asked.

"Oh, I found plenty! Hundreds of pages of stuff,

but it's all fantasy! Vaneblone didn't find nothing, not one artifact, not one piece of gold. Nothing!"

"Father, you didn't actually think you were going to find gold, did you?" asked Kate, trying to soothe him.

"Why not? I'm over fifty. My business is going down the tubes. I've dreamed of finding buried treasure all my life, and right now I could really use it. It's just not fair."

"That's very silly, Dad. You sound like a baby."

Just then Terry came in. He was worried about Reggie because he'd never had an octopus and didn't know how to take care of one.

"Terry, can't you see we're busy here?" said Dan. "I don't have time to think about your squid right now."

"He's an octopus and that contest won you fifty dollars, mate," said Terry. "You could be a little nicer. I just want to know what to feed it."

"How should I know?!" cried Dan. "What am I, Captain Nemo all of a sudden?"

"I told him fish sticks," said Craig, leaning in the kitchen eating an ice-cream sandwich. "I bet he would eat fish sticks. You got any, Dan?"

"Leave me alone."

"You should try shellfish. Crabs, mollusks, that kind of thing," I said.

"How do you know?" said Craig.

"I had an octopus once."

"Hmmmm," said Terry. "He would really eat crabs?"

"Un-huh. But he's a she. Male octopi don't get that big."

"Far out, mate," said Terry. He went to the fridge to scrounge for Reggie's dinner.

"God, this is depressing," said Captain Dan.

"Maybe you should look at the notebooks again," said Kate. "Maybe you missed something the first time."

"You look," he said. "I've had it. Vaneblone was nuts. He starts talking about ghosts and Menehune and weird magic spells. I say forget him. He's better off missing."

"Captain, sir?" I said.

"What is it, Pendleton?" Dan was resting his head in his hands.

"McKraft is a powerful guy, right? I mean, he seemed pretty smart to me. Well, if Vaneblone was just crazy and nothing he did made any sense, why does McKraft want his notes so badly?"

"That's right," said Kate. "And what about those tunnels? Arron was there, he saw them. You said Vaneblone wrote about them too."

"Let Kate and me take a look at them," I said. "Maybe you missed something."

"Watch it, kid," said the captain.

"What he means, Dad," chimed Kate, "is that maybe what we need is a fresh mind on the case.

Look how tired you are. Take a break, let us do some of the work. Please?"

Dan stared at us for a long time. Then he reached into his shirt pocket, took out a skeleton key, and handed it to me.

"Here's the key to my desk," he said. "Go into my study and read every one of those notebooks. Both of you. Don't come out until you find something of value. Preferably clues to buried treasure, but at this point I'm not too picky."

I grabbed the key. "Are we still going to the caves tomorrow?"

"It's your call, kids. Read the notes and tell me what to do."

CHAPTER 22

Captain Dan's study was a small room upstairs with a big picture window. It was crammed with stacks of paper, fishing tackle, and books about the sea. There were sextants and barometers and shark jaws hanging on the walls. An old whaler's harpoon was nailed up above the picture window.

"You'd never guess it was my dad's study, would you?" asked Kate, opening his rolltop desk.

Inside were piles of Vaneblone stuff, all the journals and diaries and drawings and letters he'd written while on Kauai. We stared at the hundreds of pages, pages that Captain Dan had already read, pages he hadn't found anything in. Someplace in there was a clue to what McKraft was after.

"Don't worry," Kate said, glancing at me over the rim of her coffee cup. "We'll find something. My dad is not the most thorough of people. I doubt he read this stuff carefully. He gets bored quickly."

"Where do we start?" I sighed.

She pulled out a leather-bound volume and handed it to me.

"This one's as good as any," she said. Then she collected half of the other papers, took them over to a clump of pillows on the floor, flopped down, and quickly flipped through several pages at a time. She didn't look like she was reading exactly— more like psychic browsing.

"What are you doing?" I asked.

"You know, trying to get a feel for it."

"It's not fair," I said. "Some of us actually have to read this stuff."

But I was joking. I didn't mind at first. It was exciting to look at real scientific notes in an actual adventurer's notebooks, but pretty soon my enthusiasm dimmed. It was nearly impossible to make out the smudged chicken tracks and crude drawings. Some were written in pen or pencil, but most were scrawled in things like crayon and black chalk. The parts I could read were Vaneblone's "theories" about ancient Hawaii. Anthropological stuff about spoon making and medicine men and human sacrifice.

Then Vaneblone got paranoid. "They are after me," he'd scribbled. "They don't think I know they're out there, but I can sense them. Man, or Menehune, I can sense everything, like a jungle animal. At night I sharpen my dagger and gaze into my campfire. Where are they hiding? I'm so close to finding it! When? WHEN WILL MY SEARCH BE OVER? . . . "

I put the notebook down and rubbed my eyes. There was still a stack of diaries piled up and waiting for me. The task seemed hopeless.

"Find anything?" I asked.

"Not yet . . ." Kate said, chewing on her pencil.

"Why did your father get so upset when I told him about McKraft?" I asked, remembering how the captain had exploded when he heard the name. "They didn't know each other, did they?"

"Not really," she said. "It's a very old story. . . . "

"What?"

"Well, my father holds McKraft responsible for the death of my mother."

"Oh no, I'm sorry. I didn't—"

"I don't know all the details. It was fifteen years ago. My mother was almost full-blooded Hawaiian, a real island woman. She was kind of a political activist, very committed to preserving

Kauai's ecology. It used to get her into trouble. One time she tried to stop one of the big hotels from going up on the south side. They were blasting with dynamite and stuff and she was killed in the explosion. That was one of McKraft's first hotels."

"I'm sorry. I didn't mean to . . ." I said.

"It's okay. It was an accident. Of course my father doesn't see it that way, but. . . . Better keep reading, or we'll never get through."

I opened another book from the pile and discovered Vaneblone's bug collection. He had pressed dozens and dozens of bugs between the pages like wild flowers, and taped a name and a number next to each one. Spiders, I was revolted to see, were his favorite. It was a disgusting hobby.

"If you think his notes are bad, look at this," I said, holding up a page of dead spiders with multicolored crayon descriptions about each one.

"That's gross," mumbled Kate, without really looking up.

"I'm beginning to hate Alistair Courtenay Vaneblone the Third," I said.

Then Kate sat up like she discovered America. "Hah!" she yelled, smiling for the first time in an hour. "Hah!"

"What hah?" I asked.

"What do you mean 'what hah'?"

"You said 'hah' twice. I was curious what it was in reference to."

"'Hah' means I found something. Something worthwhile in this mess. Listen. February twelfth. He starts talking about Davis Falls, see that? Then he says he's got to hide 'it,' whatever 'it' is, and how Davis Falls would be a good spot.

"Then, on the thirteenth, he goes into town for supplies. He goes to the hardware store—here's a receipt, see?—He bought a shovel and a pick ax. He was going to bury something! Only he doesn't say what or where exactly. Just Davis Falls."

"It doesn't make much sense—"

"No, Arron, listen. We can safely guess, after your meeting with McKraft, that Vaneblone must have come across something McKraft wanted very badly. McKraft must have been after him and he had nowhere to hide the thing. So he buried it out in the middle of Kaalau Valley—to keep it safe till he could take it back to England. But he was killed before that ever happened."

"So what is it?"

"What is what?"

"The thing. The thing he buried."

"I don't know."

"But what—"

"Shhh—I'm thinking."

Kate went back to work through the books. She made some notes on a pad, chewed some more on her stub of a pencil and concentrated hard wrinkling up the bridge of her nose.

Personally, I'd had it with reading Vaneblone's notebooks. I didn't have that kind of concentration. My mind drifted to other things, like it did in school when it looked like I was reading or taking notes but I was actually thinking about something totally different.

Suddenly I was aware of where my mind was headed.

I'd been thinking about Kate. About how ALONE we were, up in her dad's study.

I got nervous.

I knew I should say something, but I couldn't think what. My throat was dry. Say something nice, I thought. Say something cool—but all I could think was how beautiful she was just sitting on the floor, on that pillow, and how I loved the way her nose crinkled up like that, and I wondered if she was thinking about me at all, and what it would be like to kiss her . . .

"Wow," was all I said, standing there with my coffee cup in both hands like a moron.

She stopped her work suddenly and looked at me.

"What?" she said. "You want to kiss me?"

I completely froze.

My brain went dead and my fingers loosened their grip on the mug, tilting it and sending a stream of coffee down on my bare feet.

"I didn't say anything," I said. "I mean, I said

'wow.' That's all. Just 'wow.'"

"But you did. You—you said—" she blurted.

We looked at each other for one endless, panic-stricken moment. I wanted to die.

"I—I'm sorry. I'm sorry," she stuttered, and ran out of the room, leaving me in a pile of dry-pressed spiders.

CHAPTER *23*

E*arly the next morning* Dan woke us up and wanted to know what we had decided. Kate told him we should pack up and go to Davis Falls and look for something—she didn't know what—buried there. Excited by the word buried, Dan rustled up the crew, and before I knew it we were on the water, sailing for the Na Pali Coast.

Kate and I were civil to each other but we were both so mortified about last night we couldn't really speak. She wouldn't even ride in the same boat with me. I was in the lead Zodiac with Captain Dan, Craig, and Sammy, while she followed with the others. Dan kept glancing at me, then looking over his shoulder at the other boat with Kate and Spartacus sitting up in the bow like hood ornaments. I could see he was upset.

My cave was the first stop. We trekked up there so Captain Dan and his crew could see it with their own eyes. It wasn't easy to find as I'd only been up there once, and I'd been lost at the time—not to mention chased by dogs and men with guns.

"This is the way," I'd say, leading the gang through the underbrush. Everyone was tired and no one seemed in the best mood. Then we'd hit a dead end or I would change direction suddenly, saying, "Sorry, sorry, this is the way. I'm sure this is right." This didn't improve anyone's disposition.

"Are you sure now, boy?" grumbled the sweating captain.

"Yes, this is it," I said.

"Are you sure you didn't imagine the whole thing, boy?"

"No, sir, I did not imagine it. You'll see. I think we're almost there."

Once we found the waterfall and I showed them the cave behind it, they changed their tune. And after we climbed in and had a good look around, they were ready to kiss my feet.

When we were back outside, Captain Dan patted me on the back—whack, whack, very hard and painful. It was his idea of a friendly pat. He was feeling a good deal better. It was as if he could smell his treasure, somewhere out there in the valley.

"All right, gang, let's get together here," said

Dan, hitching up his shorts. "We've got a lot to do. Let's just get organized here. Kate, dear, are you ready?"

"Yes, father, dear," she said.

"After you, then. By the way, how about saying a congrats to the wonder boy?" He tried to wrangle his daughter over my way. "That's quite a find he made, ain't it? I might just call him captain, from now on. Captain Hawaii. What do you think, Kate? Why don't you say thanks?"

"Drop it, Dad," she growled, and started back down toward the beach.

The Zodiacs sailed again, this time to a remote end of the Na Pali Coast where we anchored the rafts and left tough old scarred-up Sammy as a guard. Here was the gigantic Kaalau Valley, overgrown with jungly forests and circled by jagged green spear points—the Na Pali Mountains. It was beautiful but deserted and spooky. I wouldn't want to be left there alone like Sammy was.

We followed Kate, since Davis Falls was all her idea and she was the only one who even sort of knew where to go. For an hour we trampled through the forest, Captain Dan whining, "Are we there yet?" every five minutes and Kate saying, "So far so good." It was the same broken record for two whole miles, until we finally got to the falls.

Kate stopped and pointed. "Thar she blows."

It was a sorry-looking little waterfall, pouring

into a swampy thicket.

Instantly the whole crew was grabbing for tools and scrambling up the embankment like a pack of apes. Captain Dan fought his way to the top, poked around in the leaves with his shovel, then gave up. He went to the edge of the waterfall and glared down at Kate in frustration.

"This is it? This? It's a mud puddle!" he said.

"Is that the thanks I get?" she asked.

"Would you two please get up here and help us find what we came all the way here to find? This place is a mess."

Kate continued to ignore me as we climbed to join the others. They stood in the mud watching her, shovels gripped like rifles. She stared at the ground, looking serious.

"Any ideas?" asked Dan.

"I'm thinking. It's hard to concentrate with everyone staring at me like that."

"Everyone, turn around!" said Dan, impatiently. "Give her some privacy!"

Everyone turned around and gave her some privacy.

"Okay, where is it?"

"Gee whiz!" said Kate. "How the heck should I know? It could be anywhere."

"This Davis Falls thing was your idea, Kate. I'm counting on you. We're all counting on you," said Dan in exasperation. "Are you concentrating?"

"Yes, of course."

"So, where's the treasure?"

"I'm not Superman, Dad. I'm doing the best I can. I'm thinking."

"Why don't we dig the whole place up, then?" asked Terry.

"Without coordinates, that would take days," said Vance, the know-it-all man.

"Kate," said her father, trying to be patient, "what about the journal? Is there anything more in there? Something you missed maybe?"

"No, Dad, this is all it said. Look, everybody, I have to say I think it stinks the way you're making this all my problem. And you know how I feel about this treasure business. It's materialistic. It's selfish. You're acting very greedy."

"You're absolutely right," said Dan. "And we will all apologize—after we find the goods. I promise. Anything come to you yet?"

"You should be ashamed!" she said. "You're all acting like children. Even if I did know where it was, I wouldn't tell you now."

With that, she climbed down the falls and sat cross-legged on a rock in the water, eyes closed tight. It looked like she was meditating. The case was closed.

Dan was crushed.

"Well, that's that," he said. "There'll be no

changing her mind now. She'll be there for hours if she wants to be."

"Great. Now what are we going to do?" said Craig.

Dan looked at me. "Got any bright ideas, Mr. Pendleton?"

"Me?" I asked. "Gosh, no. I guess I could look around, but I really don't think it would do any good."

"Couldn't exactly hurt, could it?" he said, stretching out a hand in invitation.

"You mean just pick a spot and dig? Just like that?"

"Say to yourself, 'If I were going to hide buried treasure, where would I hide it?'"

"And then just dig? Just on my guess?"

"Why not? You found the caves."

"The caves were an accident," I said. "I didn't want to find them, believe me."

"That's not an accident, that's luck." The captain was getting a little desperate. "You've got the touch, kid, and right now we need it badly. Please, just point your lucky finger at some spot and say 'dig' and I won't ask anything more."

I looked at the mess of mud and trees and vines. I wouldn't have a clue where to bury treasure here. I wouldn't have a clue how to find it again if I did bury it, either. Maybe I wouldn't make such a good Captain Hawaii after all.

"I don't know," I said, dejected.

"Come on. Our Captain Hawaii can do it, I know he can," prodded Captain Dan.

"Okay," I said, pointing to what looked like the best spot. "Over there. I'd hide it over there."

"No, son, no," said Captain Dan, shaking his head. "That's solid rock, see? Can't bury anything there. Don't be embarrassed, now. Just try again."

I pointed to another spot under a big banyan tree.

"How about there?" I said.

"Where? Here?" said Dan, running to the tree, shovel ready.

"Over more to the right. Between the two big roots."

"Here?" he asked.

"Yeah, I guess."

"Don't say, 'I guess.' Say the word."

"Okay. Dig."

"You better be right," he said, with a wolfy smile. Then he raised his shovel and struck down—CRUNCH!—Immediately the ground crumbled and Dan disappeared under the tree in a rain of dirt and stones.

"I guess he found it," said Vance.

"Captain!" I shouted, and ran to the hole, feeling awful, since I was the one who picked the spot.

"I'm all right, I'm all right," said Dan from

somewhere under our feet. "There's something down here. I'll be damned, there's something down here! Flashlight!"

Craig turned on his flashlight, threw it down the hole, and hit Captain Dan square in the eye.

"OW! Be careful, for crying out loud!" he yelled. There was a pause, then he started scraping around like a mole and soon handed up a green metal canister about three feet long. He surfaced next, huffing and red-faced, covered in dirt. He spat the flashlight out of his mouth, leaned back on the jungle floor, and caught his breath.

Inside the canister was a strange and very old map that no one could read—just an old picture of the island, badly drawn, with red, curvy lines running all over it. It was rotting slightly at the edges and it smelled funny.

There was a long silence with bowed heads, like someone had died. Dan tried very hard to hide his disappointment. He'd wanted to find gold very badly.

"I'll be," Dan said. "Would you look at that."

"It's a map," said Vance, blankly.

"It sure is. Hmmm . . . "

"It smells funny," said Terry.

"Well, it's very old," said Dan. "You'd smell funny too if you were that old."

"Are you sure that was all that was down there?" Joanne just couldn't believe it.

"Yes!"

"This is so completely ridiculous! I can't believe we wasted an entire afternoon for this," said Craig.

"Well that's helpful," snapped Dan. "That's nice and helpful. I didn't see you complaining while I did all the work."

"Well, what are we supposed to do with the thing?"

"Bring it to Mama Kauai," said Kate, who had stopped meditating and now stood behind us with her hands on her hips. "Mama Kauai will know exactly what it is."

CHAPTER 24

We covered the hole—just in case someone came snooping around. Then we sat by the waterfall and ate lunch. Dan gave me the map to carry since, he said, it was technically my find and none of this would have been possible without me. Not that he cared much. The map wasn't worth a dime to him, but it was a nice gesture.

I told Kate how delicious my tofu sandwich was, that it was the first tofu sandwich I'd ever eaten and that, in fact, I would never have believed you could make a sandwich out of bean curd. I was basically trying to break the ice that had formed last night, but she was still being a little cold. That plus the general mood of gloom within the group made for a pretty quiet lunch.

We were done eating and had started packing up, when Kate stopped suddenly and put a hand to her ear. "Shh," she said.

"What is it?" said Vance.

"Shh, I hear something," said Kate.

"I hear it too," said Joanne, standing up and listening hard.

"What?" said Dan. "What's it sound like?"

"It sounds like . . . "

"Drums," said Kate.

Then we all heard it, very faintly at first, then steadily louder. Sure enough it was drums. Beating somewhere in the jungle.

"I got a real bad feeling about this," said Craig.

"That's very, very odd," said Captain Dan. "Where the hell is it coming from?"

"Who the hell is it coming from?" said Craig.

"They're getting closer, guys," said Terry.

Then I heard something else, something worse. A wispy, moaning sound. It started low, like the drums, then it grew into an awful, choking howl— a horrible noise echoing down from the hills.

"We better be going!" shouted the captain. He quickly grabbed all his tools. "Terry, let Sammy know we're on our way."

"What's going ON?!" I yelled, but no one answered. The noise was so loud we could hardly hear. Everyone was scrambling to get their gear together, and Terry loaded up his flare gun with a bright orange cartridge.

"It's the bleedin' Menehune, I bet," he hollered and fired the gun, spitting a sizzling flare up through the trees into the bright sky.

"Menehune?! I thought . . . They're just make believe. . . . They don't really—"

"Come on, kid, move it!" shouted Captain Dan. He grabbed me by the collar and started sprinting, Kate and the others followed. This was a different trail—more direct, but steeper and muddier. We ran crazy fast, ducking under vines, jumping over logs. The drums pounded through the forest, getting louder, getting closer. My heart thumped like mad. I was terrified of spraining my ankle and getting left behind. Dan was pulling me along, charging faster than I could go. I gripped the map canister with sweaty hands.

Down the slope through the trees I saw the beach and the boats. We were almost safe. Sammy would be revving up those engines. Just another half mile. . . .

"How ya' holding up, boy?" shouted Dan.

"Okay." I wheezed.

Dan turned his head around, taking his eyes off the trail for a split second, looking to see if Kate was okay. At that exact moment, as we charged down the trail faster than seemed possible, I saw, glinting in the sun, the thin, shiny cord stretched tight across the ground.

A trip wire!

I remembered the booby trap from the other day and with a shock, I realized—

"Dan!" I shouted, shoving him out of the way. Unfortunately, when I pushed him, Dan let go of my collar. I shot forward, tripped the wire, and—

SNAP! went the wire. Something else SNAPPED in the bushes, off to my right.

"GET DOWN!" everyone shouted behind me. I just wasn't fast enough.

CHAPTER 25

They call it the Malaysian swing trap.

Basically the idea is that some unsuspecting moron—like me—trips the wire. This triggers a big wooden plank or log or spike to come whipping out into the trail, killing the victim or making him wish that it had.

Whatever they used, it swiped me right across the head.

I was off that trail like a rocket, barely conscious but awake enough to feel that prickly feeling in my guts that tells you you're flying.

I sailed up and off the trail, arms flailing, brain doing a stupid little dance in my skull. When I crashed through the trees, the muddy ground seemed to come up out of nowhere. . . .

I remember coming to a few times and seeing worried faces floating above me. Then I'd pass out again and dream I was falling. I don't know if I was delirious or what, but I do remember drinking tea or putrid broth, something that tasted like gerbil shavings. Then I really passed out, stopped moving, even stopped dreaming. There was just this blue nothingness for hours and hours.

Then I woke up.

I felt not good. Sick actually, like someone had replaced my stomach with a big cold fish that wasn't totally dead. My right eye was puffy and throbbing, my legs were tingly, and I couldn't shake the sensation of hurtling through space. I sat up and lay down again. Then I tried once more, slowly. My head felt like a tetherball.

I was alone in an empty room with bare walls and bamboo mats on the floor. It was still day. There was a bandage above my bad eye, and I was wearing a kimono that wasn't mine and that I'd never seen before.

"Hello? Anybody? I'm in here, awake, if anyone cares!"

No answer.

I got up slowly. I opened the sliding door and peered out into the living room of a little house. It was spare and clean, with white walls and paper windows. A big Buddha sat on the floor by the far wall.

"Hello?"

No answer.

In the kitchen, chopped vegetables lay on the cutting board and water boiled on the stove, so I knew somebody was home—only who? Whose home?

Someone was coming now. I heard flip-flops slapping on the back porch, and for a second I panicked. I almost ran, but I felt too darn sick to run anywhere.

The back door slid open and in walked Doctor Gomasio carrying a laundry basket.

"Eh! The New York Boy!" he shouted happily as he put the basket down. Then he went to the stove and dumped the vegetables into the boiling water.

"How are you feelin', Arron san?"

"What's going on?" I asked. "What happened? What is this place?"

"It's my place," said the doctor.

"What am I doing here? Where did everybody go?"

He frowned, squinting his eyes so I could hardly see them. "They went to a party, I think."

"A party?!"

"A birthday party, hei," he said, nodding sharply. "Captain Dan san brought you here so I could help you out. He says you broke your head, bad. He is very worried about you, but I told him you'll be fine. Kate, on the other hand . . . she is not so worried about you."

"I could have guessed that. Why aren't I in a hospital? How could they just go to a party and leave me like this?"

"I don't know," said Doc. "How are you feeling?"

"Kind of shaky, but okay. What happened?"

"You fell on your head, that's what happened."

"Something hit me, I remember that. My parents are going to love this."

Doc laughed at me.

"It's not funny," I said, defensively. "They're going to kill me. I mean it, they will actually take my life."

"Okay!" said the doctor, clapping his hands and rubbing them together. "This is cooking up good, so now let's take look at you. Come."

I followed him out onto the back porch where the sun poked spears through my eyes and into my brain. My headache was deadly. Gomasio told me to sit on the steps, then removed my bandage and cleaned the cut on my forehead with a washcloth dipped in tea.

"Hold still." He dabbed on antiseptic and I winced.

"Not too bad. You're gonna be okay."

"Thank you," I said glumly.

"You feel stiff?"

"Yeah."

"Good. Lie down. Here." He pointed enthusiastically to a foam mat on the porch.

"I really appreciate all your help," I said, "but I should get going. My family will start to worry and, well, you know—"

"Hey now! I'm the wise Japanese shiatsu-massage-sashimi-surf-master. Just sit still and do what I say. Anyway, Daniel san made me promise to get you into fine shape so you can go to the party. Lie down."

"I'm not going to the party," I said. "And I don't want a massage. Really."

"Fine. Lie down."

"Listen, I really don't want any—"

"Lie down. Don't worry, it's not gonna hurt."

It hurt like crazy. He jammed his elbows into my spine and crunched his knuckles into my shoulders, pulling and kneading and stretching till I thought he'd kill me. I had to bite down on a towel to keep from screaming.

"Too much tension," he muttered.

"This can't be good!" I yelped, digging my nails into the floor. "Why does it hurt so much?"

"Ahh. Finally you ask a real question. About time. You carry too much tension in your body. This is poison—very, very bad. Massage releases this poison and that is painful. But it leaves you relaxed and healthy. Strong, so you can apologize to Kate san."

"What?! What are you talking about?"

"Apologizing to Kate san."

"Right, I know that, but why? What the heck should I apologize to her for? I didn't do anything."

"You must have done something. She's pretty mad at you."

"Oh, fine. It's my fault. Great. Well, you know what I think? I think this is crazy. I think everybody on this island is one hundred percent crazy. You're all nuts. I've been here a few days and I've got people trying to kill me, my parents think I've lost my mind, and you people are mad at me? You all need mental help—I don't even know you people!"

I tried to get up.

"Look," I said, "let me just get out of your way, and go about my business. Then you can go about your business and everyone will be happy."

But I wasn't going any place. The doctor had me pinned to his porch with his powerful arms.

"Where are my clothes? You can have the kimono back, just let me up, okay? I'll just take my clothes and go."

"Your clothes are in the washing machine," he said quietly. "They were covered with mud."

"Can I please go? Please? I appreciate everything you did for me, I really do. I feel better now. But I really want to just go and get out of everybody's hair. It would be better. This was all a big mistake."

"Where will you go?"

"Back to the hotel. Where I belong."

"McKraft is there."

"I'll take my chances. Better odds than sticking around here. Besides, my parents are there."

"Running back to your parents. Hah!" he said.

"What's that supposed to mean?" I said.

"It means you are a coward."

I writhed to get away from him. "My life has been in perpetual danger, in case you haven't heard."

"You're making a mistake."

"SHUT UP! What do you care! You don't know anything about me!"

"Hmmm," he said. "I know you. I know that all your life you dreamed about adventure, about something different, something better, heh? So, you come to Kauai and now you have it—but you're scared. Maybe that's understandable. Maybe. But you're turning out a coward. Why? You don't trust enough. You don't trust yourself. You don't trust Kate san. You don't trust me.

"Listen, Arron san, everybody comes to Kauai for a nice vacation. Everybody comes here to take and take, but soon there will be nothing left. Tourists take. McKraft takes. You take. Soon everything will be gone. Kauai is a magic place, Arron san. But soon it will be dead. No more magic. You must learn to give back, to listen, but not with your head—don't listen with your head, heads are no good. Listen with your heart. What does a heart tell you?"

"I don't know," I said.

"Love!" he shouted. "LOVE! Simple."

"But I just—"

"No BUT! What do you do when you love something?"

"I don't know—"

"You become responsible."

"Responsible for what?"

"I told you!—the egg test. Remember?"

"What are you driving at, because I really don't—"

"Stupid," he said. "Why did you catch the eggs?"

"Because you threw them at me," I said.

"NO! No. I threw *to* you. At you is a different test."

"Okay. Because you threw them to me."

"Aha. See?"

"See what? What does that mean?"

"Just because I throw an egg does not mean you must catch it! Suppose I'm a crazy person, are you responsible for that?"

"Yeah, so?" I said. I was expecting more. "That's it? That's the test?"

"Maybe."

"What about the eggs, though! It doesn't matter who threw them. I didn't catch them."

"Ahhhhhh," he said. "Very good. You failed the test."

"Wait! But you just said I wasn't responsible for someone else throwing eggs!"

"BUT," he said, "IF YOU FEEL A RESPONSIBILITY TO EGGS, THEN YOU MUST DO EVERYTHING IN YOUR POWER TO CATCH THEM!"

Something was beginning to make sense. Deep in my head a bell was ringing, telling me to pay attention because maybe this wasn't such a load of garbage after all.

"Correct me if I'm wrong," I said, "but you're not talking about eggs really, are you? This is like a Zen thing, right? The eggs are supposed to represent something else."

"Hmmm," said Doc. "Now that's a start."

"You're talking about Kate Pierce, then. And the map. And this whole crazy thing with McKraft. Right?"

He stopped digging in my back and sat back on his knees.

He did know me. Somehow, someway, he knew more about me than anyone. They didn't call him doctor for nothing.

"So what do you think I should do?" I said, after a long pause. This really exasperated him.

"I'll give you hint, stupid boy. This map is no joke. Kate san takes it very seriously. She's a stubborn girl, like her father—and she gets in trouble, like her mother. You apologize. You help her. Face it, you're here for a reason. Don't run away like a big chicken boy."

"She read my mind and now she hates me," I said.

"Hei, I know."

"She knew how I felt and I denied it. I guess that was a pretty crummy thing to do, wasn't it?"

"Hei, pretty crummy, Arron san."

"What if she really doesn't like me, though? And if I apologize I'll have to admit all that stuff I was thinking when she read my mind. I don't know if I can do that."

"Why not?"

A breeze blew off the garden and I took a big breath of flowery air. I was feeling better. My head didn't hurt anymore.

"Then I'll apologize," I said. "What should I do first?"

The doctor frowned and scratched his crew cut.

"Flowers would be nice," he said.

CHAPTER 26

When *I felt up to it*, I called my parents to say I'd be late, then Doc and I crashed the birthday party. We drove to the Sheraton Hotel in his old VW Bug, and marched down to the pool, where the party was going strong. I felt funny carrying that bouquet the doctor had recommended. And I felt really dumb wearing his fancy kimono, but that was really all he had to lend me. My clothes were still in his dryer.

There was a band playing and people were dancing or wandering around eating chicken off paper plates. The party was for some guy named Mokie, whom I never met and never even saw—I just know his name from the banners that read HAPPY 50, MOKIE. Doc assured me no one cared what I was doing there, or what I was wearing. "And besides," he said, "you look fantastic." Then he left me by the buffet tables and wandered off into the crowd of guests.

"Hey kid, nice outfit." It was Craig, chewing a shrunken hot dog off the end of a toothpick. "Glad you could make it, pal. Hungry?"

"No, thanks," I said.

"How you feeling? Doc said he'd have you ship-shape and over here in no time. Said you'd look worse than you really were. Hey—nasty bump on your head there. Does it hurt much?"

"Not too bad, no," I said. "I've felt better, though."

"I bet you have. Seems you're always getting beaten up, kid. What is it with you? You had us pacing the floor. Hey—what's with all the flowers?"

"Oh, these?" I said. "Nothing really."

"Ohh, I get it. Kate, right? Trying to win her back, eh?"

"Just an apology."

"Yeah. I know those apologies. Are you in love with her, or what? You can tell me, I'm her uncle."

"Give me a break, will you please?"

"You got it. Come on, I'll show you where we're sitting. Dan's over there now, waiting for you. Honestly, I've never seen him so upset in my life as when you got clobbered this afternoon. Really. Should have been him, he kept saying. He's been worried sick about you."

With a beer in hand and a jaw full of pretzels, Dan looked anything but worried sick. He had pillaged an entire table for his Zodiac pirates and there he sat, showing off for the attractive tourist ladies. They lounged near him, hanging off his arm and laughing at his jokes, which were worse than ever. He wasn't drunk—just comfortable in his skin, and he greeted me like a long lost brother.

"Feel okay?" he shouted. "Boy, that was some

beating you took out there today. Glad to see you up and around."

"Thanks. Glad to be up and around. Why did you all leave me and go to a birthday party?"

"Some luau, ain't it?"

"Oh yeah, it's great," I said. "But my question is why are we here?"

"It's more than great!" he continued, not answering my question. "This is a real honest-to-goodness Hawaiian luau. No tourist baloney. Just smell that pig. That's the real thing." He pointed down to the beach where shirtless men were roasting the poor thing in a pit.

"By the by, Arron my friend," said Dan, leaning in to whisper in my ear, "to answer your question, we are here because I made an appointment with Mama Kauai tonight. To show her the you-know-what. She's running this shindig, so we'll just have to wait until after the hula show. Then she'll see us. But not a word to anyone. Those flowers for my daughter?"

"Yes, sir."

"Good. You'll need 'em. Look, I'm sorry for whatever happened. She's a stubborn girl. I tried to talk to her, but your name's mud as far as she's concerned. Where the hell did you get that bathrobe?"

The music stopped and soon our table filled up with the rest of the Zodiac crew. They all made jokes about my outfit.

I kept my eyes peeled for Kate, getting oozy inside and wondering if I really had the guts to give her the flowers. . . . If she really, absolutely hated my guts, in the sincerest way, then she wouldn't want my flowers. She would laugh, she would—

Kate sat down next to Joanne, as far down the table from me as possible. She didn't glance at me, didn't say a word—not even about the kimono.

I was hyperventilating.

My hands fumbled with the flowers under the table. She'll kill me, I thought.

"Excuse me," I said. "Excuse me, please. I have something I need to say."

"Everybody hush up," called Dan. "Mr. Pendleton has something to say. What is it, boy?"

"It's to your daughter, actually," I said. "It's personal, but I was afraid she wouldn't talk to me in private, so I'm going to say it now. Kate, I uhh . . . "

"Go on, boy," prodded Captain Dan. "Do what you gotta do."

"Kate, I umm . . . I can see you're angry and you have every right to be, but please hear me out. We all know the last few days have been crazy—at least they were for me. I've just been confused and not thinking real clearly.

"I guess I'm apologizing, here. This is an apology. What I did was crummy and I'm sorry. I never should have lied like I did, even if you did kind of read my mind. So, basically what I'm trying to do, what I'm trying to say is . . . uh, that all the things I thought I meant. I like you a whole lot. I mean really a real lot. So . . . forgive me. Please. If you want to."

I walked over and gave her the flowers, then stared at the tablecloth, since it wasn't going to stare back.

Silence.

Not a sound from anyone for a thousand years. Then Kate stood up, gulped down Joanne's drink, wiped her mouth with her sleeve, and said, "Excuse us, please. This is a private matter."

She led me far away from the party, past the roasting pig and down to the edge of the surf. We were alone pretty much. The music and party laughter faded in the twilight.

Kate turned on me suddenly.

"What's the big idea?" she said.

"There's no big idea. I meant what I said."

"I don't like these games," she said. "I don't know what you're used to in New York, but it's not going to work on me."

"Kate, listen, please. I talked to Doctor Gomasio. He gave me some advice. I understand better now."

"He put you up to this? Why is everyone on your side?"

"He's not on my side," I said, exasperated. "He

thinks I'm pathetic! I was going to run back to my parents. Ask him."

"It isn't so easy for me, you know," she said, turning away.

"I know."

"No, you don't. I'm different. I scare people. You think it's easy having special powers that come and go? Do you think I enjoy being den mother to my father's crazy friends?"

"I never thought that."

"Of course you did. I seem so damned confident, nobody thinks that I feel anything, that I have the same, ordinary feelings as anybody. I'm just boring and ordinary."

"I don't think so," I said.

"Okay, then I'm a freak. You think I'm a freak, just because I have a little problem with my ESP."

"No!"

"Don't lie, Mr. Pendleton. I can tell, remember?"

"All right. At first you scared me, I'll be honest. But Kate, I didn't know any better. Everything on this island is different from the rest of the world, like another planet. You've got to give people a chance to adjust."

"That's just it," she said, and now she was crying. "I don't want adjustments. I want to be like everyone else."

"No, you don't," I said. "You don't know how

good you've got it."

"I'm alone. It doesn't matter how special you are, if you feel alone, you're alone. I've never even had a boyfriend."

"Neither have I," I said. "I mean, a girlfriend. Nothing special anyway. It was always awful."

"I'm blonde," she said.

"What's your point?"

"My point," she said, sounding angry, "is that you like blondes. You thought I was cute and you're only here for a week. I'm just a good story for your friends in New York."

She walked back to a row of beach chairs and sat down. I stood a few paces away, under the palm trees. The first dim stars were just rising over Hanalei Bay.

"I never thought you were cute," I said.

"You didn't? Never?"

"Nope."

"Flattery will get you nowhere," she said.

"Look, if I told you how I feel, you wouldn't believe me."

"Tell me anyhow," she said.

"You already know—you tell me. It's like I've known you for years already, like we grew up together or something. It's got nothing to do with you being some beautiful girl, which you are—let's be honest. But there's nobody else like you. You have some kind of magic life—I'm not saying easy, but it's magic. You make everybody happy, just by being around them. I just got here and I'm already depressed that I'll have to leave, because then you'll be nine thousand miles away."

It was hard to tell in the deep twilight, but I think she blushed. Then she stood up and came toward me, closer and closer till her lips were pretty much in cinemascope.

"Hold it," I said. There was something moving behind a hala tree down the beach, and it caught my eye.

"What?" she said.

"Were you . . . ?"

"Was I what?"

"Were you going to kiss me?"

"I'm not sure. The thought did cross my mind."

"Not now," I said, stepping back and peering into the darkness.

"What's the problem, why?"

"Because I think your father is spying from the bushes."

With a laugh, Captain Dan stumbled out of the thicket, hiding the binoculars behind his back. "Don't mind me, kids," he said, winking. "Go right on about your business."

"Dad, I am going to kill you!"

"Later, sweetie," said the captain, running backward away from his angry daughter. "First we see Mama Kauai."

CHAPTER 27

We *waited forever to see Mama Kauai.* The hula show seemed like it would never end. Each time the drums stopped, we thought our chance had come, but another group of dancers would leap up onto the rickety stage and start shaking. Captain Dan paced and looked at his watch till he simply couldn't stand it anymore. He got us and went behind the stage, went right up to Mama Kauai and stood there, frowning.

Lying back on her chair, she watched her dancers and sipped on a very tall mai tai. She was not happy to see us, and she looked furious when Dan bent down and shouted in her ear.

"Mama, I'm really sorry, but you promised to give us a few minutes, remember? Normally I could watch hula all night long, but unfortunately I got kind of a time problem."

Mama Kauai shrugged and motioned us all forward with her finger. She was a tough woman and it scared me a little, the idea of bothering her. There was something about her, some power, some fierceness in her old eyes. . . .

"This will only take a second, I promise," continued Dan. "You see, we found something buried out in Kaalau Valley, Mama. We think it might be important, but we just don't know what the devil it is. Katherine here, she said we ought to bring it to you since you're so wise and all—"

"Thank you, Kate, dear," said the big woman. "If only your father was smart like you."

Dan laughed nervously. "Yup, you can say that again, Mama. Kate is the smart one in the family."

"Don't bore me, Daniel Pierce. You said this . . . business . . . it only take a second. Hurry up."

"Yes, yes," he said, "right away."

Kate and I opened the canister. We unrolled the parchment and held it flat. The old woman slipped on her bifocals, squinting to see in the flickering torchlight.

She looked at the map for a second. Then her eyes got huge and she leaned forward, dropping her mai tai and moving her shaking hands like she was going to grab at the map or tear it with her long nails. She looked horrible.

Kate and I pulled away, scared of her, and scared she might fall over from a heart attack and we'd get blamed for it. Instead, she stood straight up, straddling the lounge chair.

"Where did you get this?!" she cried. "Tell me, where you got this!!"

"I told you, Mama. It was buried out in Kaalau Valley," said Dan. His face was stretched with concern.

"BURIED?! How did you know where to look?!" shrieked the woman. She was enraged—or something about the map frightened her terribly.

"The kid found it," stuttered Dan, pointing to me.

"Don't drag me into this," I said.

"He found Vaneblone's notebooks. There were clues. What's the problem, Mama?"

Suddenly the old woman was like a wild animal. She lunged for the map, forcing us backward into the sand.

"Give me the map!" she hissed. "GIVE IT TO ME!"

"Tell us what it is first!" said Kate.

"It's nothing! Nothing but worthless garbage! Now give it to me—it's mine!"

"Not so fast, Mama," said Dan, snatching the map and rolling it back into the canister. "We found it, we keep it. For now. If it turns out to actually belong to you, you'll get it back, but not until we do some checking."

Mama Kauai was shaking with rage.

She raised her fat hand and pointed a lava red fingernail at my nose. "Mama Kauai is warning you, boy. You're in some deep water. Anything happens—anything bad—it gonna be all your fault!"

CHAPTER 28

Once again I called my parents to say I'd be later than I thought, and once again they gave me guilt for spending so much time away. They weren't exactly mad, but they wanted me back, for one whole day anyhow. Captain Dan nearly threw a fit. He warned me not to leave tonight, that my hotel was too dangerous, but I wanted to keep my parents happy.

I caught the last shuttle for the Blue Egret and got there by ten. I went to the pool immediately, found my family all there, lounging in the moonlight, a crinkled stack of magazines by their side.

"Well, well, well," said my father over the rim of his *Wall Street Journal* as I approached. "Judy, look who's back."

"Oh, my," she said, "Arron, dear. Did you have a good time? We missed you. You got a lot of sun, Arron. Are you wearing sunscreen? Look at you, in a kimono. My heavens."

"You're going positively native on us, son."

"That is, without a doubt, the gaudiest thing I've ever set my eyes on," said Lisa, not smiling, not even looking up.

Robby could not stop laughing. He thought I was wearing a dress. Tracy thought I looked very pretty. I was mortified, but luckily the kimono covered my collection of bruises, and my baseball hat, tipped over my left eye, hid the worst of the big scab on my forehead.

"What's that mark, dear, on your head?" said my mom. Mom radar—sees all things.

I made light of it. "Just a scratch. Hiking accident. That volcanic rock is sharp, you know."

They asked me a billion questions about my day and about Kate. They thought she was "enchanting," as my father put it—"enchanting girl" he kept saying.

They had no idea how crazy things were, or what danger I was in—which meant they also couldn't know how much fun I was having. I assured them I was having a fine time and that Captain Pierce was taking excellent care of me. I tried to make it sound like Dan was some important guy, that I was lucky to be "working" with him. I made it out to be real oceanographic and ecologic so they'd think I was learning something.

In the morning Robby and I went to the pool and horsed around. We had this game called knife fight that wasn't much of a game really, just an excuse to beat each other up. How it went was, we got into the water up to our necks and we each pretended to have a knife. That was pretty much it. Then we'd lunge at each other and wrestle around until one of us got mortally stabbed.

There was always a lot of screaming and

inhaling water and coughing for five minutes. We had fun for a while, till Robby kicked me in the place where we had promised not to kick each other, and the game was over.

"I'm sorry," said Robby. "But you grabbed my neck and I thought you were going to drown me."

"I wasn't going to drown you," I wheezed, slouching down onto a plastic pool chair.

"You killed my shoulder," he said, making like to kick me again in the same place.

"Do not even pretend to do that," I said, "or you will lie down and beg for death."

Tracy came up behind me and put her hands over my eyes.

"Guess who?" she demanded.

"Godzilla," I said.

"Nope. Guess again."

"Charles Darwin?"

"The Creature from the Black Lagoon, dummy," she said and stomped around with her arms dangling out in front of her, like a monster.

"I kicked Arron where it counts," boasted Robby.

"Where does it count?"

"None of your business," I said. "I'm going to the steam bath, I'll see you later."

"I'm coming!" she screamed.

"You can't come," I said. "Ask Lisa to take you to the girls' steam bath. This one's only for guys."

To reach the spa you had to go through a silly man-made mountain where the middle part of the pool went inside a big fake grotto. There was a phony waterfall and a rope bridge where kids spat gum down on the older people swimming laps. There was even a bar in the grotto, so you could get a drink right there in your wet bathing suit and fall back into the water.

I was walking over the bridge, trying to wedge past all the screaming children, when I happened to look down at the bar. What I saw stopped me dead.

Of all the people in the world, who should be down there slurping away at some frozen pink beverage but the greasy-haired thug who blew up Captain Dan's Zodiac. And who should be toasting him but Vance Viebermann, Captain Dan's own trusted friend.

I felt my heart shrivel to the size of a pea.

How could this be? Vance was on my side, wasn't he? He was a Zodiac pirate, one of the good guys. Why would he hang around with scum like that?

Something was very wrong.

I turned away and made a bee line for the spa. They hadn't seen me, so I took a moment to lean against the wall and collect the thoughts that raced like hamsters through my brain.

Why would Vance be drinking with the enemy,

with a Stingray, with a McKraft stooge?

The answer was obvious. Vance was a traitor.

As I took a long drink from a water fountain, out of the corner of my eye I saw two men round the bend and come down the hallway toward the spa.

It was them! They were laughing like they were best friends.

I had to go somewhere, fast. The gym was at the end of the hall, but I couldn't go there. It was one big, bright room, with nowhere to hide. The only other place was the spa. I ducked through the glass doors, ran past the locker room, and went in the next door I saw, the one marked steam room.

A thick wall of white vapor boiled out from a bed of rocks in the floor. Clouds of steam filled the room and I had to grope my way around. I climbed up four rows of tiled bleachers to the top where it was hottest. The steam folded around me like hot silk sheets.

I waited.

I thought.

They'd never come in here.

The door opened and I heard Vance's voice. They were here! Not even fifteen feet away!

"Are we alone?"

"Seems like it," said the greasy thug.

I heard Vance come closer. He must have been looking through the fog to see if they had company.

As he climbed up the bleachers toward me I pushed myself flat against the hot tiles, trying to be as small and silent as possible.

He was six feet from me . . .

Five feet, but looking the wrong way.

If I can hardly see him, then he can hardly see me, I thought. Maybe he'll miss me . . .

"Hello?" called Vance. "Is anyone in here?" He sounded like Schwarzenegger.

Please don't turn around, please don't see me, I thought, rivers of sweat and water rolling off me. Is it possible to dehydrate in a steam bath?

"I think we're alone," said the slimy guy.

"Yah," said Vance.

I heard one of them fiddle with the door—probably jamming it shut. As I huddled there, they began to talk. I could hear every word.

"How much, Jack?" said Vance.

"Five thousand. Even exchange," said Slimy Jack. "That means you have what I want, and you're by yourself. Alone. Comprende?"

"How do I know the money is good money?" asked Vance.

"C'mon man, that's bogus. My boss has a reputation to keep, even with guys like you. He's not into games. I should be asking you that question. How do I know that map is real?"

The map! Vance was selling us out for the lousy map! Five thousand measly bucks! Why did everyone want that thing so badly?!

"I promise, Jack. It'll be the same one we found. I'm not stupid."

"I'm sure you're not. So . . . let's say midnight. Tonight. Banzai Pizza. Be there or be dead."

"Same goes for you, Jack."

"Hey, man, Mr. Mckraft doesn't joke around. He wants this thing ended and if it doesn't go right tonight he ain't gonna be happy. Things will get rough. For you, for Dan Pierce, for his cute little girl. And definitely for that haole punk from New York. Keep that in your brain."

CHAPTER *29*

Things were hopping at the Tropical Deli. Kate and Dr. Gomasio were back at work, feeding all the folks who washed up on their door with two dollars and an appetite. The place was full up with surfers, Rastafarians, and all the folks that time forgot. They looked at me like I was strange when I came rushing in off the shuttle bus, screaming for Kate.

She was making vegetarian lasagna and trying to serve three customers at once, but she dropped everything when she saw the look on my face.

"Well, hi there!" she said. "I thought you were staying at the hotel today, buster."

"So did I. My parents are not thrilled, to say the least."

"Hey, what's the matter? Did something happen?"

"It's Vance," I said. "We got a big problem."

Doc took charge of the deli while Kate and I went back to the stockroom where I told her about the conversation in the spa. She made me sit down and drink tea while she called her dad. He raced over from the office, and I had to tell the whole story again.

Dan went through the roof. He was furious—and vengeful. I ate a burrito while he called Craig, Terry, Joanne, and Sammy. They all raced over to the deli from wherever they had been. Then I had to tell the whole story a third time, then again, because Terry never understood anything if you only said it once.

Kate went back to work and I helped her, washing dishes and other simple stuff that even I could do. She was worried that her dad might go off and do something stupid—something dangerous. She cared about the map, but she was pretty much a pacifist and didn't want anybody getting hurt over it, even Vance. She told her father this before he stalked off, but he wasn't in the mood to hear it.

"What do you want me to do?" he said, stealing a clump of dried apricots from a glass jar on the counter and stuffing them in his cheek like chewing tobacco. "You want me to just forget this ever happened? Sweetheart, something's fishy on this island and the smell is coming right from McKraft. We can nail this guy, but not without the map. Without that we have nothing."

"No violence," said Kate. "That's all I ask. Hey! Take it easy with the apricots, Dad. They don't grow on trees, you know."

"That's exactly where they grow," said Captain Dan, snatching another handful. "Okay. No violence. I promise. But I'm stopping Vance. And I'm gonna be at Banzai Pizza tonight too. You're not going to be involved, so don't worry."

"Oh, I'll be there," she said. "Someone's got to keep an eye on you."

Dan left without paying for the apricots. I went with him.

First he got the map canister and replaced the map with a bunch of those coiled-up spongy worms, the kind that pop out of a can and scare people. Then he put the canister in his footlocker, up in the loft of the hangar, where he often kept valuables. That would be the first spot Vance would look, he was sure.

When that was done, he went home and hid the map in his underwear drawer. I had to admit, a safer spot he could not have found. I'd never look around in there, anyway.

Then we just had to wait. Dan parked his truck

in the alley by the hangar to watch for Vance, and I went back to the deli. When he was ready he would call us for help on his walkie-talkie. The only person who was not going to help was Dr. Gomasio. He refused to have anything to do with Dan's plan, or the map. He just made sushi and laughed at us. Can't say I blame him. I didn't want to help Dan either, but Kate was going to and I wasn't about to stay behind like chicken boy if she was out there being brave.

At five o'clock we got our signal—Dan's voice screaming out of Kate's walkie-talkie.

"Hey! HEY! Do you read? Is this thing on? Man, I almost missed him. He's going into the hangar now. Let's move it! Let's go! Where's my backup?!"

We dropped the lasagna and went tearing out into the street toward the Ching Yung Shopping Village, almost crashing headlong into Joanne and Terry as they came bounding through the arcade carrying rope and rolls of tape. Terry also had a baseball bat.

Craig and Sammy saw us go by and brought up the rear. They charged out of Banzai Pizza with deluxe slices in their hands and long strands of melted cheese trailing out of their mouths.

Everyone still had their walkie-talkies on and Dan was still screaming curses over the airwaves, scaring the tourists. They leapt out of the way as we came running, parting like the Red Sea.

We rounded the corner into the alley and saw Dan hiding in a doorway and peering at the hangar with his binoculars.

"What took you so long?" he said.

"What a question," huffed Kate. "I'd like to see you run that fast."

When we burst into the hangar Vance was up in the loft, holding the empty canister. Dan stared at him for a long time.

Spongy worms were everywhere.

"It was a lot of money, Dan," said Vance, finally.

"Five thousand dollars is peanuts," said Dan.

"Enough to fix up my boat and sail out of this dump," said Vance, sadly.

"You never did like this island, did you?"

"No, I didn't. I'm sorry, Dan. I really didn't think this map business mattered. I'm glad you're taking it so well."

"Like hell I am," said Dan. Then he ordered us to lock the exits.

"You're lucky you were never good enough to work for me, Vance. Because if you were one of my pilots and did this to me, to my daughter, you wouldn't have a prayer. You'd be shark bait. You were just supposed to be a friend, not a pilot, so you can relax. Now get down from there."

Vance slowly climbed down the wooden ladder and turned to come toward us.

158

"That's far enough," said Dan.

"Oh, come on, man. I'm not going to do anything."

"Don't talk to me. You can tie him up now fellas."

"Wait a minute," said Vance. "This is me you're talking about. You don't gotta tie me up."

"Yeah?" said Dan. "And I didn't have to hide the map from you either, did I? Don't come any closer, I told you . . . "

Vance had his hands up, looking very hurt and like he learned his lesson.

It was a good act.

"Please," he said. "Please, Dan, try to understand my position here . . . "

"I said do not move. Tie him up guys—come on!"

The pirates were so uncomfortable seeing big strong Vance acting like such a baby, they didn't have the heart to restrain him. He came closer, holding his arms out and begging for mercy.

"Please, Dan—"

"Tie him up!"

Vance wasn't even five feet away, when he stopped, turning to me and smiling mean.

He knew.

In a flash he lunged at me and grabbed a crowbar off the workbench with his free hand.

"It was you!" he shouted. "You little rat!"

I whirled around to get away from him, but he kept coming, swinging the crowbar like a club. He grabbed my shirt, ripping it clean down the back. I grabbed at the counter to try and steady myself. Tools and equipment went flying.

The pirates were on top of Vance, trying to pull him off me, but Vance was a moose of a guy—bigger by far than any of them. He threw them off and came at me again, this time catching me around the waist. But he was off balance and we toppled to the floor like dominos.

Now all of us were splayed out on the cement, the pirates grabbing at Vance's kicking legs, Vance ripping at my shirt and belt, and me desperately clinging to the legs of the workbench, sharp tools clattering down around my head.

Finally they stopped him and hauled him off me. He was screaming bloody murder as they tried to tie his legs and arms.

"You should have let me do it, you should've let me! You idiots, you can't fight McKraft!"

He struggled right up to the point when Dan knocked him out, and he was still yelling as he slumped over into their arms.

"Pendleton—you won't make it off the island . . . you . . . little . . . brat."

CHAPTER *30*

So *far, things were going along* as planned. We still had the map, no one was too badly hurt, and Vance was locked down in Sammy's boat, giving him plenty of time to think about what a bad boy he'd been. The rest of us had gone back to Captain Dan's house, where we just sat around looking gloomy. Finally Kate had had enough and said she wanted to get out of there, so the two of us got in her car and drove into Hanalei.

It was raining, one of those north shore downpours, hard enough to dent the tin roof of the Blue Dolphin Restaurant. All the geckos came inside and ran upside down on the ceiling, holding tight with their sucker toes. No one seemed to mind them. I couldn't wait for one to slip and fall into someone's salad.

"Tell me more about New York," Kate said. "Does it snow on Christmas? Do they have a jazz club in the Empire State Building?"

"Hold it," I said. "Before we get into that, I need to get some things straightened out."

"Okay, like what?"

"Like everything," I said. "Like what the heck is going on in every way? Why does McKraft want the map?"

"I don't know."

"What were those drums in the woods yesterday? And who sets up those booby traps, and why?"

"I don't know."

"Why does Mama Kauai want the map?"

"Don't have a clue."

"What is the map? No. Don't tell me. You don't have any idea."

"Not really, no."

"What happened to your amazing brain?" I asked. "You're supposed to know all those ESP things."

"One more crack and I'll stab you with my lobster fork, I swear."

"I know, I'm sorry. Just a joke."

"My amazing brain can only pick up on things if they're very strong, like feelings. I don't automatically know everything in the universe. All I know is, there's a lot more going on here than we imagine.

"I really don't know any more than you, Arron. But my guess is—and don't laugh, I stayed up all last night thinking about this—but my guess is, it's the Menehune. Maybe the map shows you how to get down inside the volcano, where they live."

"They're real?" I asked, thunderstruck. "I thought they were just, you know, stories."

"I've never seen a Menehune," Kate said, sadly. "I'd like to. Mama Kauai believes in them, but she says only pure-blooded Hawaiians are ever allowed to see them and I'm only part Hawaiian, so . . . "

"Yah, but she's a little nuts—"

"Don't say that, Arron!" said Kate, grabbing my arm. "She might have family here. Besides, she's a Ho'okalakupua. You shouldn't talk about her like that."

"She's a what?"

"I thought you knew," said Kate. "Ho'okalakupua. It's like a witch. No big deal."

"She's a witch?"

"Shhh!" said Kate. The waiter was approaching our table with dinner plates in hand.

"I have an idea," I said, changing the subject. "Why don't we ask Dr. Gomasio? I bet he would know what's going on."

"Oh, I'm sure he does," said Kate, squeezing lemon on her opakapaka. "Probably knows as much as Mama Kauai."

I was shocked. "He does? Well, why doesn't he do something, then? Why doesn't he tell us what's going on? I don't think that's fair."

"It's just not his kind of thing," Kate said casually. "Now tell me—is there a jazz club in the Empire State Building?"

After dinner we waited on the porch for the rain to stop. In the background, the neon restaurant sign buzzed like a giant fly. It was getting late and I was worrying about part 2 of Captain Dan's Revenge.

"Thinking about tonight, aren't you?" Kate asked.

"How'd you know?"

"Stop asking me that. Do you have a creepy feeling, Arron?"

"What do you mean, 'creepy'?"

"I mean, something's slightly strange, like something's gonna happen."

"Yeah," I said. "You too?"

"Yeah."

"Oh, great. Now I'm really scared. Are you actually going through with this?"

"Got to. Can't let my dad do it alone. But you don't have to, Arron."

"If you're going, I'm going," I said.

Just then, with no warning, she kissed me. Right there under the porch, in the rain.

"What was that for?" I said.

"Because I like you, stupid. And if we both die tonight, I won't get another chance for a long, long time." She hugged me.

Over her shoulder I watched the neon blue dolphin blinking in the rain. He seemed to stare at me, with a big smile on his fishy face. His electric blue nose curved over his tail and pointed down Route 56, toward the mountains hiding in the black night.

164

CHAPTER *31*

"**Y**ellow Ferrari," I whispered into the walkie-talkie.

Sitting back-to-back with Kate on the roof of the Ching Yung Shopping Village I had a good view of both the plaza and the street where the car pulled up. We'd been there for at least forty-five minutes. The rain was just stopping and it was dark and wet and uncomfortable. But it was a darn sight better than being down in the plaza where the others were. No bad guys would be up on the roof.

"Ferrari? Over," cracked Dan's voice from my walkie-talkie. He was hiding somewhere in the shadows of Banzai Pizza.

"It's a Lamborghini," corrected Kate.

"Sorry. It's a Lamborghini," I said.

"Midnight, exactly," said Dan. "Listen, don't forget to say over when you're done talking, or things will get all screwed up. Is he alone? Over."

"Sorry. Yes, he's alone. Over."

"Is he armed? Over."

"I don't know," I said, trying to see through the mist. "He's wearing a jacket."

"Over?" asked Dan.

"Over, yes, right."

Kate pointed across the street where a van had

pulled up and parked in front of the Hanalei House of Mystery Museum. It was the Stingray Cruises van, the one with the flames.

"Hold on," I said. "We got a van too. It's just parked there. Over."

"Can't do anything about that now," said Dan. "Just forget 'em. Proceed as planned. Over."

Slimy Jack stepped out of the Lamborghini and started walking toward the plaza.

"He's heading your way. Over."

"Which direction? Over."

"The end closest to the supermarket—the far end from you. Over."

"Good," said Dan. "End transmission. Over."

Slimy Jack walked into the plaza. He whistled as he sauntered toward the pizza parlor, his footsteps knocking on the pavement, knock-echo-knock.

He checked his watch.

He got closer.

Suddenly, Dan and Terry appeared from behind a giant wooden pizza sign. They stood under the street lamp, looking pretty mean and serious even from up where I was.

Their words came crisp in the stillness.

"Name's Jack, isn't it?" said Dan. "Vance couldn't make it."

Slimy Jack showed the teeth under his sunglasses, kind of like a smile. "Stupid, Mr. Pierce.

166

Very stupid," he said. "What do you want? You want the money? It's Mr. Viebermann's money. He was smart, you know. It's always the smart ones who abandon sinking ships. Or is it stinking ships?"

"It's rats, moron, like you," said Terry, slapping the baseball bat in his open hand.

"Five thousand wouldn't pay for half the Zodiac you blew up," said Dan. "If you had twenty thousand, I might take that."

"So the deal's off, I guess," said Jack. "Is that why you gentlemen came here tonight? To tell me that?"

"Nope," said the captain. "Two other reasons. First to give you a message for McKraft."

"Which is?"

"He's messing with the wrong bunch. The map is ours, and it stays ours till we find the rightful owner, which is not him."

"And reason two?"

"To make you promise never to be a bad boy, ever again."

Up on the roof, Kate whispered, "No violence . . . he promised!"

"Kate, don't do anything. I bet he's bluffing to just scare him," I said.

We watched Slimy Jack turn tail and run back toward the car. He got halfway down the plaza when Craig and Joanne popped out of the trees in front of the Kauai Yogurt Shop.

"How's it going?" said Craig.

Slimy Jack stopped short, slipped and then fell right on his rump. He started shouting, pathetically calling out for help. The Zodiac pirates came at him in the darkness and lifted him off his feet. Then Dan grabbed him by the collar and shoved him against the wall. It looked like there might be some violence after all.

Kate backed away from the edge of the roof and shut her eyes.

Slam. The van door slid open.

Three Stingray goons stepped onto the street.

They started walking toward the plaza.

I grabbed the walkie-talkie and flicked it on. "Hello? Hello?!" I whispered. "Get out of there! You've got company." But there was no answer. Dan had turned off his unit.

"What do we do?" Kate said.

"I don't know."

I looked down into the plaza. Dan was wrestling with Slimy Jack, slapping him around good—probably trying to make him talk. If Dan didn't let him go, if Dan didn't get out of there right away, those thugs would get to the plaza and there would be a real fight. Maybe with guns and knives.

"Let him go, Dad—" whispered Kate.

I wanted to shout, to warn them—

"Let him go, Dad—let him go, let him go—"

"I knew this was a lousy idea. We have to do something, Kate," I said. "Someone might get killed!"

Pata-pata-pata-pata. The goons walked in their flip-flops, across the street . . .

"We gotta do something, Kate!"

"Hold on one second."

Pata-pata past the mailbox on the corner . . .

"Kate—"

They were on the sidewalk . . .

"KATE—"

"One more second, Arron."

Slimy Jack's backup goons were at the parking lot, moving through the puddles of lamplight on the wet asphalt, when something strange appeared out of the shadows.

It was a tiny Pekingese dog. It came down the sidewalk, pulling itself forward with tiny, little legs, and barking like a fiend.

Then there appeared a long leash . . .

a fat hand . . .

an arm . . .

and finally the whole of Mama Kauai herself.

She waddled right out in front of the goons and blocked their way. She was quite a sight with her red muumuu and cane, smoking a huge cigar.

The goons stopped short.

"Excuse me," said Mama Kauai. "This dog is al- ways wanting to go out late, when nobody's around. . . . What are you boys doing on my street this time of night?"

"We got business here, Grandma," said one of the bozos.

They started moving again, trying to get past Mama, but she was mad now. She wouldn't let them by.

"Great-grandma to you, sonny," she said.

Then she lifted her heavy cane and jabbed the guy hard in the stomach.

"Oooph!" he said and collapsed, writhing in pain.

Next the tiny dog sprang into action, leaping on the second thug, and clamping its jaws into his knee.

The third idiot just hung his jaw down about a foot and stared at the old woman. He was shaking and took timid steps backward across the street.

"WOT?! BODDAH YOU?!" shouted Mama.

"No, I, I . . . " said the guy, but it was too late for an apology. Mama Kauai raised her cane and pointed it like a shotgun.

"E Pele-honua-mea, e la!" she shouted, and in a blast of purple smoke, the poor fool was rocked off his feet and blown across the street into a rack of garbage cans. Magic or not, it was quite an impressive sight.

The pirates all heard the noise and came rushing into the parking lot. When they saw Mama

Kauai standing there with one Pekingese and three big thugs all stretched out and groaning on the ground, their jaws dropped.

Mama looked at them for a while, puffing on her cigar. Then she started to chuckle.

"Don't bother thanking me," she said.

Then, turning around, she kept walking her dog down the street, blowing smoke rings over her shoulder like nothing happened.

I was gawking, my eyes like Ping-Pong balls. "W-what? H-how . . . ?"

Kate just smiled coolly, as if she knew all along Mama Kauai would come to the rescue. "You can relax, Arron," she said. "We can get down now."

"I'm exhausted," I said. "I have to go back to the hotel and go to sleep."

"My dad can take you. Hey, cheer up. I told you everything was going to be okay."

CHAPTER 32

The next morning when I got to Kate's house, the pirates were still asleep on the living room floor. Kate, wide awake and newly showered, was busy making pancakes. I helped her as best I could and then she blasted a tape and woke everybody up with her favorite Benny Goodman swing music. Soon the kitchen was crowded with groggy pirates, scratching, yawning, and shuffling in and out of the bathroom.

Dr. Gomasio showed up, explaining that he smelled our breakfast all the way across town and he just couldn't pass up Kate's pancakes. Nobody could. She must have flipped a thousand of them. We just kept eating and eating and drinking coffee and eating, until we all ended up lying around the living room holding our guts.

Eventually talk turned to the map and Dan started his usual pacing and beard scratching.

"We can't just sit here and wait, that's for sure," he said. "We've got to think of something to do. Anybody got any ideas?"

"We could research," I said.

"What?"

"Research. We could research the map, go to the library, get some books on Hawaiian history. If the map is real, there might be some reference to it somewhere."

"Good thinkin'. I like that," said the captain. "That's the kind of thinkin' that gets us places. There's also defense to be considered. It's only a matter of time before McKraft puts the pressure on us, especially after last night. We gotta figure how to defend ourselves."

"Against McKraft?" Craig snapped.

"Sure, why not?" said Dan. "He's just a guy, an

average Joe. He's not unbeatable. Don't be a downer, Craig."

"Doc," said Kate, "you've been awfully quiet over there. What are you thinking?"

"Yeah, what's on your mind, Doc? What've you got rolling around up there?" asked Dan, suspiciously.

Gomasio smiled. "Nothing much," said Doc. "Maybe only one thing. Try to figure out what enemy will do next. Try to keep a step ahead."

Dan nodded and chewed some pancake. "Good point," he said. "So, what will happen next?"

The doorbell rang.

Joanne got up to answer. When she came back a minute later, she was as white as paper.

"Umm . . . there's some people here, Dan," she said with a shaking voice.

"Who is it this time, for heaven's sake."

"It's L. B. McKraft. He wants to come in."

"Well, well, well," said the big man in the white linen suit. "What a charming place you have here, Daniel. Very rustic. Very homey." McKraft raised up his arms in a fatherly manner, as if to hug us all. He was brimming with cheer and goodwill. He seemed calm and totally at ease, but that's probably easy if you've got two bodyguards outside the door and a caravan of cars parked in the driveway.

We all just stood there looking pretty shabby and dumb.

Dan was boiling mad but he did his best not to show it.

"This sure is a surprise," he said. "We weren't expecting you."

"I know, I know, it's rather sudden," said old L.B., touring around the living room. "It's a pity I didn't do this a long time ago. Hello there, Mr. Pendleton. It's good to see you again. I've been meaning to call you about having dinner, but you're a hard man to track down. How about this evening?"

"I don't know, sir," I stammered. "I may be tied up."

"I suppose you want to sit down," said Dan, pulling some sheets off the couch and throwing them into the hall.

"Thank you, yes," said McKraft, stretching his heavy legs out with a sigh. "Are those pancakes I smell, by any chance? Golly, I bet they taste good."

"Uhhh, yeah. You're hungry?" said Dan.

"Famished, actually. Had a board meeting this morning and didn't eat a thing. Silly of me. Breakfast is supposed to be the most important meal of the day."

"I've heard that," said Dan. "Kate, would you get Mr. McKraft some breakfast?"

"That would be just great, thank you much,"

said McKraft. "Please call me L.B., won't you?"

I went to the kitchen with Kate, who silently heated up the griddle and made another batch. I brewed the coffee.

"Got any rat poison?" I said, but she didn't even smile. When we brought the food out, everyone was sitting around talking painful small talk, and smiling nasty, fake smiles. McKraft dove into his food with gusto and couldn't stop saying how good it tasted, over and over again. I couldn't believe what was happening.

Finally, when things had reached the peak of all-time weirdness, Dan broke the ice.

"Well, L.B., what is it exactly that you want?"

McKraft wiped his long, thin lips and pushed the plate away with a deep breath.

"Well, Daniel," he said, "as lovely as this visit has been there is a matter that concerns both of us . . . and, although I hate to bring up business after a delicious breakfast like this, I . . . well, I really must."

"Go ahead. What's on your mind."

"It's come to my attention that my company, Stingray Cruises, has been involved in some acts of unpleasantness with your own company. Unpleasantness verging on violence—"

"Verging isn't the word I'd use," said the captain.

"Well, you understand how hard it is to find

good help these days. I don't run the company, you know, I simply own it. But I guess the young pilots today can't be trusted to operate a company. They're a rough bunch. They have no respect. Had I known earlier you've been suffering harassment, I would have made this apology sooner."

"An apology, eh?" said Dan, his blood starting to simmer.

"I'm ready and happy to offer a husky chunk of money as an apology, yes. That's why I came this morning. I was shocked to hear the details of what's been going on. I'm truly sorry."

He was hamming it up like the pig he was, trying to look all nice and loving to his fellow man.

"Money?" said Dan.

"Yes, sir, money. Sixty thousand dollars. More if that's not enough. Zodiac boats are expensive, I understand."

"You understand right, mister," said Dan. "But don't tell me—there's one more thing, right? One little thing you want in exchange? Let's cut the nonsense here and now. You want to buy the map from me for sixty big thousand bucks. That's a lot of money, which means that map must be really worth something more to you."

"Excellent arithmetic, Mr. Pierce."

"So let me take this one step further. You take the map. I get the money. Then you—and correct me if I'm wrong—but you then turn around, try and steal the money back, then destroy me and my company. In all honesty, L.B., I don't like the idea. Actually I think it stinks."

"The map is mine, Mr. Pierce. It belongs to me."

"If the map was yours, you wouldn't have to use sneaky, dirty little tricks to get it back."

The room was silent while the two men stared at each other. You could just see the bad blood between them. It got so tense, Spartacus skulked under the coffee table and whimpered.

"I came here in good faith, with an honest offer," said Mckraft. "I take it you refuse?"

"You bet your behind I refuse."

"Very well, then. You will not be given a second chance. That is the final word."

"No, it ain't," said Dan. "You owe my daughter five bucks for the pancakes and coffee. We ain't running a soup kitchen, you know."

While McKraft dug in his pockets for the money, he looked at me like we were friends and had some understanding. "Don't bother calling about dinner, Mr. Pendleton. I'll just assume you're coming. All righty?"

He left ten dollars and told Kate to keep the change.

CHAPTER *33*

While *the pirates grumbled* and thought of all the places they should have told McKraft to stick his lousy sixty thousand, there were constructive things to do. First, Kate and I went over to Mama Kauai's Bar to thank her for last night. I didn't really want to go, but Kate made me. She said it would be rude if I didn't come along, no matter how scared I was of the old woman.

The bar was closed that early in the day, but the bartender knew Kate, so he let us in and took us upstairs. Mama's office was in the dark, back part of the hall. There was no door, just a colored bead curtain. We knocked on the doorjamb but Mama didn't invite us in. She talked to us from somewhere inside, while we stood in the rickety hallway.

She didn't talk much, either. Once Kate got through with thanking her, Mama just heaved a fat sigh and said, "No trouble." But then, after a pause so long it seemed like she'd fallen asleep, she said, "You bring my map, Katherine?"

"Mama, I can't give you the map," said Kate. "I want to, I really want to be fair. If it's yours we'll give it back, but we have to be sure who it belongs to first. Mama, my father is in trouble. McKraft is going to put him out of business. Dad's got no money and he's too stubborn to change, but the map might—"

"That map maybe more trouble than you can handle, Kate, dear," said Mama Kauai. "Some plenty trouble. Mama stay one tough old great-grandma. Mama knows how to go and deal with such things. That map very good and very bad. Let me keep it safe away." She was doing something back there, snapping cards down on a table it sounded like. Smoke from her cigar puffed through the bead curtain.

"What about you, Pendleton boy?" she said as if she could see me, even though I was hiding flat against the wall and hadn't spoken a word. "I owe you money o' wot?"

"Me? I don't understand."

"How come you all the time stare at me but don't say nothing? Ever see a witch before?"

"A witch?"

"Yes, a witch. A Ho'okalakupua. You one sly mongoose, you tell Kate to go and give me my map. You can't read it anyway."

"I can't tell Kate to do anything," I said.

"Too bad. Shame," she snorted. "'Cause if McKraft gets hold on to that magic, then he's a Ho'okalakupua too. And that will be bad news for everybody."

"McKraft? A witch?" said Kate, but there was no answer and I couldn't hear anything from

179

inside anymore. Kate boldly peered through the beads into the darkness.

"Mama?" she said. "Mama?"

I tried to stop her, but she was already on her way into the office. "Kate, don't—"

"Come in, Arron. Look."

I poked my head in. There was an old desk with a deck of cards laid out and an old lamp with a painted shade. Mama's cigar sat, half-burnt and smoking in the ashtray. But the old woman was nowhere to be found.

It was still morning when we went to the beach. Haena Beach is down at the end of Route 56, right by the trailhead. It's a long stretch of sand, near some woods that are fun to creep around in. We did that for a while, then sat in the sun on the towels Kate had stashed in the back of her car. Then we went swimming, ignoring the sign that said WARNING—DANGEROUS CURRENT.

It was great. I was minding my business, having a relaxing swim off a deserted beach. I wasn't asking for trouble, I wasn't mouthing off, when all of a sudden here comes this Zodiac splashing around the bend and spinning to a stop not five feet from me. Driving it was of course Slimy Jack, with his newly cracked lip and two black eyes. They weren't my fault, but he was going to make me pay for them anyway.

Kate was on the beach. She had seen the boat first and started screaming for me to come in. I thought she was screaming about sharks or tidal waves—all I heard was something like "Arron, get out of the water, now!" My head was so filled with saltwater I couldn't hear much, which is why I didn't start swimming till the Zodiac was looming over me, blocking out the sun, with Slimy Jack and his thugs reaching over the side to grab me and pull me up.

I was surprised. I mean, it scared the life out of me, them sneaking up like that, but I guess that's the point of a kidnapping. I was shouting and kicking and clawing and cursing almost as bad as Captain Dan. Kate was screaming too, and running hopelessly into the water, but she couldn't do a thing. They had me stuffed inside some huge canvas duffel bag and thrown down onto the rubber floor of the Zodiac before I could catch my breath.

Just for the record, you know in movies, where the hero gets blindfolded and taken miles out of the way—then he figures out where he is just by listening very carefully? Forget it. It doesn't work.

CHAPTER 34

"Where is he, boys?" said the familiar voice.

"Over here, sir. We'll get him for you."

I heard a pair of feet shuffle over. Hands picked me upright and stood the bag on end. Then the zipper opened and the bag peeled away, leaving me squinting and shivering in my wet bathing suit. I was inside someplace, but I didn't know what someplace.

"So glad you could make it," boomed the voice. As my eyes adjusted I saw L. B. McKraft towering over me, arms outstretched in his typical way. He was wearing an ugly tuxedo.

"What do you want with me?" I chattered through my teeth.

"My dear boy, just the pleasure of your company. I wanted to have you for dinner, remember? Purely a friendly thing. A social get-together."

"You should try sending invitations. They're a lot easier for everybody," I said.

McKraft laughed and his bow tie went up and down with his Adam's apple. Real attractive.

"Well, you're not easy to get to know. This way I knew you'd come. You must be freezing, look at you." He draped a bathrobe over my shoulders, which helped—but why did I keep winding up in other people's bathrobes?

"What do you think?" he asked, nodding around at his office.

I looked around. Pretty ritzy—lots of wood paneling and brass, like in a ship's cabin. There was a giant painting of fish on one wall, a huge conference table, and a huger desk with his precious artifacts and children's books. There was no sign of Chinese food, but for some reason, everything smelled like Peking duck.

"Lovely," I said. "Really very special."

"Truly?" he said.

"Yes, truly."

"What do you think of the carpeting?" he asked, staring down at the rug and rubbing it with the sole of his polished shoe.

"Carpeting?"

"Yes. They just put it in, but I'm not sure about the blue. Powder blue. My wife likes it, but . . . "

"It's more like aquamarine," I said, squirming. "Goes with the ocean stuff you've got going. Listen, I don't want to be rude, but where am I and what do you want?"

"That's not rude, boy," he said, striding over to the fish mural. "That's a damn fine question. This is where you are—"

He pushed a button and the painting slid up like a garage door and disappeared into the wall, revealing a fish tank. If you looked past the monstrous fish, you had another view—a Chinese restaurant, as gaudy and overdone as McKraft's hotel.

"Wow," I said.

"Yes, wow," he said. "Welcome to the China Palace. Finest dining on the island, as the advertisement claims. It's true too. I know because every darn thing you see is mine."

"It figures," I said.

"So that's where you are," he continued, coming over and placing his meaty mitts on my shoulders. "As for the 'why,' well, I think you can guess."

He offered me a drink and a cigarette, which I refused. He didn't refuse, so he poured himself something over ice and blew stinky smoke all over the place.

"I'm not a bad man, Mr. Pendleton . . . "

"I never said you were."

"I know, let me finish," he snapped. "I'm not a bad man, but some people give me a bad reputation, some of your friends. We don't share the same views politically—you know the way it goes. But my belief is that they just don't see the beauty of my dream. They aren't smart enough to look at the future of this island and see that the wildest, most wonderful things are possible."

He puffed a few times and waited for these great words of wisdom to sink in.

"Your friends mean well, but they don't know the whole picture. They are happy the way they are. They don't want progress. They don't want progress for anybody. But progress isn't something that can be halted, my boy. It has a life and a mind of its own. You don't run from it and hide your head in the sand, mumbling about so many trees and a couple of endangered species. You jump on, you ride progress like a bull, you make it to the top like I did. You do that, or you get crushed."

Another pause and more smoking. His eyes were popping wide below his eyebrows. A loony, I decided. Crazy as a nut bird.

"So what's this got to do with me?" I asked. "I'm just passing through—"

"You're a visionary too, Mr. Pendleton."

"I'm fifteen years old," I said. "I'm on vacation with my parents. That's all I am."

"Don't argue with me!! You're a visionary, you just don't know it. You've seen places. You've seen the map. You've seen magic things."

I said nothing, but I was thinking about all the things Mama Kauai said, and thinking that she might not be so crazy after all.

"You don't think a man gets to be where I am just by working hard, do you? Sometimes you must step on somebody. Sometimes you have to use anything you can get your hands on—for the sake of progress, you understand. I'm not above trying a little hocus-pocus . . . "

"What exactly is it that you are talking about, if I may ask," I asked.

"I'm talking about the future of this island, boy," he said sternly. "I'll show you."

He walked over to the middle of the room and pushed a button on the side of the big round conference table. Immediately the center of the table slid away and something started to rise up mechanically and rotate till the thing stood as tall as me. I quickly realized it was a model of Kauai, perfectly detailed—only there was something different about it. Something very wrong.

There weren't any farms or sugarcane fields. No deserted beaches or parks or crooked hiking trails. Not one square inch was natural.

The lights in the room dimmed and the model began to spin a little faster. From a hidden speaker came sounds of shouting and laughter and wild carnival music. The entire island was transformed into one gigantic amusement park. Hundreds of theme hotels junked up the beaches. Shopping plazas sprouted up all over the south shore. The whole north shore blinked with lights and snaked with a hundred roads. There were Ferris wheels spinning, helicopters taking off, arcades, and a thundering loop-the-loop roller coaster charging its way in and out of lava caves, with what looked like tiny screaming passengers waving minute hands. It all seemed practically real.

"You haven't seen the half of it," shouted McKraft. He gave the button a second push.

Suddenly there was a noise like a volcano erupting, and the miniature island split in half like a melon. Inside the core of Mt. Waialeale, tiny hang gliders soared down to land on the roof of a sprawling hotel-casino. There were nightclubs and bars, a tunnel of love, a "haunted" forest, and miles of water slides—my water slides—rushing through the caves. But the best, most awful part was that sign rising up out of the Na Pali mountains— HAWAIILAND it blinked, lighting up the whole Pacific ocean.

"Beautiful, isn't it?!" shouted McKraft above the noise. "THIS is my dream!"

CHAPTER 35

"Give it a few minutes. Let it sink in," said McKraft.

"I don't need it to sink in, I hate it. And I refuse to talk about it anymore. I demand you take me back to my hotel."

"I don't show this to many people, you know," he said, genuinely hurt. "This is very important to me."

"I could care less," I said. "You're really nuts, you know that? You can't kidnap me. When they find out they'll lock you up. Then where would you be? That would sure be the end of your little amusement park."

"My boy, the last time anyone saw you, you

were swimming in our notoriously dangerous waters off Haena Beach. There were warning signs posted. You were off messing around with your little girlfriend. Nobody saw you leave, nobody knows where you are. If anything should, oh, accidentally befall you now, as far as I'm concerned, you were lost at sea."

For the first time I realized just how bad my situation was. "But Kate saw what happened. She saw your men. She'll call the police, she'll call the Coast Guard."

McKraft was getting impatient.

"Mr. Pendleton, I'm the most important man on this island. Who are they going to believe? Me or some wino boat captain and his flake daughter? Use your mental capacities, my boy. Now if you don't want to cooperate and get the map for me, I can always hold you for ransom. There are many ways to go about this, pleasant and not so pleasant, so what's it going to be?"

I stared at him with my most steely expression and said . . .

"No deal. You won't get anything out of me."

"Very well," said McKraft. "If that's how you want it."

He went to his desk and spoke into an intercom. "Bruno. Mylar. Bring in Fang."

Two of my kidnappers entered the room

through a hidden door, big guys with dumb faces and crew cuts. One of them carried a black Chinese box on a tray.

I had a bad feeling, like maybe I'd misjudged the whole situation, but I was too much of an idiot to say anything. I guess maybe I was frozen. Bruno and Mylar sat me down at the desk, facing that Chinese box, all without me saying a word.

"I heard that you like animals," said McKraft, patting the box gently. "You will be interested in Fang, if that's the case. Is it? You do like animals, don't you?"

My mouth was as dry as the surface of the sun, but I managed a mousy yes.

"Mylar, would you?" asked McKraft.

The even dumber-looking one leaned over, unlocked the box, and raised a little door facing me.

Nothing happened.

McKraft tapped the back of the box with a pencil.

Nothing.

"He is alive, isn't he?" asked McKraft, angrily.

"Of course he is, boss," said Mylar. "I fed him a mouse at noon, just like always."

McKraft gave the back of the box a swift smack, shoving it even closer to me. All eyes were on the little doorway. Then, from somewhere inside that darkness came a rustling noise, and two brown, hairy legs, thick as fingers, started to emerge.

I knew what it was. I tried to stand, to leave, but Mylar and Bruno held me in place. I began to tremble and turn white. I backed into the chair and gripped the leather arms with bloodless hands, but I couldn't take my eyes off the box.

Fang slowly made his entrance, hauling himself cautiously over the lip of the doorway and coming to rest, with a little thump, on the desk in front of me.

"NO!" I yelled.

Fang sensed this and pointed his front legs at me in the attack position. Fang was a hairy mygalomorph, grandson of the original Spider God, from the darkest, moldiest, remotest crevice of South America. He was an amazing creature, far bigger than a tarantula, huger still than any rubber spider in any five-and-dime magic store. He was bigger than a dinner plate.

"Fang, meet Mr. Pendleton," said McKraft, like he was introducing neighbors at a barbecue. "Fang can hunt and kill birds."

"THE MAP IS IN DANIEL PIERCE'S UNDERWEAR DRAWER!!" I screamed.

We sat down to a very uncomfy dinner, me,

190

McKraft, and his wife. Ever clever—and cheap—
McKraft had his maids steal some clothes from my
hotel room so I had something to wear to the
China Palace besides a wet bathing suit. That
wasn't considered "proper attire." McKraft said he
was sorry he couldn't get me a tuxedo like his. I
told him not to worry about it.

Mrs. McKraft read through the menu for the
eighteenth time and looked with pleading eyes for
her husband to help her order. He refused.
McKraft treated her like dirt but she got back at
him by being stupider than anyone I ever met.

"You know I need time, L.B. I never know what
to get," she whined. She had bright red hair and
was wearing about a year's supply of makeup all at
once. It looked like she'd been hit with a pie.

"Dammit, Marilyn. We own the restaurant. Just
order something. Anything!"

"You go first, then," she said.

"Oh, for goodness' sake," said McKraft. "Okay,
Arron, go ahead. What's your pleasure?"

"I'm not hungry." I said.

"Come now. You've had a big day," said
McKraft. "You must be hungry. You're my guest, I
insist you eat."

"I wouldn't eat at your greasy spoon if it were
the last dive on earth."

"Now, now, let's be nice," he said. "You don't

have to eat, but I'm sure you're famished."

I was hungry. "I'll have hot and sour soup and the Buddha's delight."

The waiter took our orders and left us. I hated myself. McKraft had made me talk and he didn't even have to lay a finger on me to do it. I had betrayed my friends because I was afraid of a spider. A very big spider to be sure, but still a lousy bug.

"Mad at yourself, eh, boy?" said McKraft. "You shouldn't be. You did the right thing. This is all for the best."

"Shut up," I said. "I don't want to have dinner with you. Why don't you let me go, or at least leave me alone?"

"Forgive me, but I find you interesting company. We may have an important future together. I shared my concept with you and I value your opinion."

"It's a lousy, stupid model," I said. "You've got a toy train in your office, that's not a concept. You're deranged. You've got awful, bloated delusions of grandeur and nothing to back them up. You're nothing. Your plan can't work. You'll never own this island. They'd never let you get away with it!"

"Son, they'll beg me to get away with it. They'll crown me king when I'm ready."

"They'll put you in prison."

"My boy, they'll make me a god."

"And how are you going to work that?" I asked.

192

"The map," he said. "That map is the key to this whole island. It is the only way to find the Menehune."

"There are no Menehune," I said.

"Oh, yes, there are, son. There are. They are my passion. I know everything about them, except how to find them. That's where the map comes in. They only come out at night—stop me if you've heard all this—they come out to do your bidding. You just have to know how to ask. I know.

"All I needed was a way to find them, and for fifteen years I searched for that map. Throughout the Pacific, Japan, China, even Mongolia. And now I discover it's right back where it started, brought here by that fool Vaneblone. Anyway, he's dead, thank goodness, so we needn't bring him into it. Tragic accident. What is important is Hawaiiland. The Menehune are going to build it for me. Kids will love it, don't you think?"

"It stinks. They'll hate it," I said. "Anyway, it's impossible."

"Impossible, eh?" he said. "This island is almost mine already. Soon I'll own everything—every major hotel, every business, every restaurant, every flower and bird and rainbow! The Na Pali Coast is mine too. No one goes camping there anymore. I have the whole place rigged with booby traps and speakers—three times a day we put on a little show—"

"The drums. I heard them," I said, rubbing the bruise on my forehead. So it was McKraft's Malaysian swing trap too. What a talented man.

"Exactly," continued McKraft. "You get the picture. I really don't understand why you're so cranky. You have no idea the kind of business I could create. Everyone will come to Hawaiiland. Even you, Mr. Pendleton. I'll give you a free pass."

He thought that would put me in my place, but it didn't put me anywhere. I was planning right then to stand on my chair and start screaming for help at the top of my lungs, but Slimy Jack showed up, sweating and pushing his way through the waiters and fern plants that hid McKraft's table from the ordinary diners.

Slimy Jack was smiling and behaving totally pleased with himself all because he had what everybody on the island wanted so badly. He waved the army-green map canister in front of McKraft's face like a carrot in front of a mule.

"Is that it?" stuttered McKraft. Then he stuttered it again, turning tablecloth white and squirting out dots of sweat onto his forehead.

"No question about it, Mr. M.," said Slimy Jack. "It was in with the underwear, just like he spilled his guts it was."

"You'll see some guts!" I said, and stood up, hitting him near as I could to his teeth. My punch didn't do much but bang up my hand pretty nicely, but I did hit him and it felt good. A couple of waiters had to step in and pull us apart before we started swinging and rolling around all over Mrs. McKraft's moo goo gai pan.

"Gentlemen!" shouted McKraft. "There is a lady present!" Then he ripped the canister away from Jack, who was about to hit me over the head with it. "Give me that!" He tore into it, unrolling the map on the table and touching it gently with shaking fingers. He was drooling with delight. "Ahhhh . . . it's the one. . . . This is my . . . my baby . . . my baby . . . my baby . . . " he mumbled again and again so that everyone, even Mrs. McKraft, started to get embarrassed for him.

I was sick to my stomach and couldn't take any more. I stood up, trembling with fear and anger.

"I've had it. I'm leaving—you can't stop me."

"Go ahead then," said McKraft, not taking his eyes off his treasure.

"I'm serious," I said. "I'm leaving—right now. See? Look, I'm going. I'm not kidding."

"You are of less than no use to me now," said the big man, giving me only one bored glance. "And it's not as if you are thrilling company."

"I'm walking out, I swear," I said, inching back away from the table, ready to run if I had to. I couldn't believe he would let me go, just like that.

The rejection almost hurt my feelings. There had to be some trick.

"I'm going," I repeated. "Don't try and stop me!"

"Mr. Pendleton, if you're not out of my restaurant in one minute, I'll have you arrested," said McKraft, nastily. "And don't forget, you owe me fifteen dollars for your Buddha's delight. It will be charged to your room."

CHAPTER 36

I *went across the street* to a Shell gas station and used the pay phone to call Kate. I had no change, so I used my dad's phone–credit card number, which he doesn't mind me using if it's an emergency. I decided this fell somewhere near the emergency category.

Captain Dan answered on the first ring, all panicky, saying, "Yes, hello, for Crimeny's sake, what's going on!?"

"It's me, Mr. Pierce, Arron Pendleton."

"Holy Smokers!" he said, then there was a clunk and an OW. "Sorry. Dropped the phone. ARRON! I can't believe it's you! Are you all right? Where are you now?"

"I don't really know. I'm not kidnapped anymore."

"We've been waiting by the phone all day, worried sick. We had to . . . to give up the map, Arron. They came right in and took it. They threatened to kill you. Don't worry, we didn't tell your parents."

"Good," I said. "Listen, Captain, it's my fault. I squealed. I let you down. Believe me, I didn't want to, but they forced it out of me."

"They tortured you?!"

"Well, not exactly tortured. There was this spider—"

"A spider."

"It was a big spider," I said. "I never saw anything so big in my life, honest. I'm sorry . . . "

"Ahh, don't sweat it," said the captain, but I could tell he was disappointed. "They can keep the lousy map. As long as you're okay."

"I wish there was something I could do, I feel terrible. McKraft is really, really—"

"He's a bad man."

"Not bad. Evil," I said from experience.

"We did our best, kid," said Captain Dan. "Now where the heck are you, so we can come pick you up."

I waited awhile at the gas station. I called my parents, but they were at dinner, so I left a message that I was fine and would see them later. Then I walked down the block and looked at the sport shops with the surfboards and scuba gear shining Day-Glo in the windows.

Kate and her father got there in an hour. They didn't say much, but Kate kissed me, which was embarrassing, in front of her father and everything. He didn't seem to notice, though.

It was a gloomy ride back to Hanalei. I told them all about what it's like to be kidnapped, and all about what I saw and heard and did. They tried to convince me not to feel guilty about the map, that it was only a matter of time before McKraft got it anyway and how he was a dirty, lousy, rotten, stinking bum and deserved to be eaten by sharks very slowly. That's what Dan said.

Dan drove us right to the Busted Schooner where we met the gang and tried to celebrate my release from the China Palace. It wasn't much of a celebration, everyone being generally too upset and angry to have fun. Dan ordered a lot of food, till the table was piled up with plates of fries and fishburgers and other stuff.

The bunch started drinking and singing and telling stories about what they would do to McKraft if they ever got their hands on him. Meanwhile I just sulked there next to Kate, who refused to talk, only stuffed her face with any food within arm's reach. I never saw a thin person eat so much in my life—she went through her dinner, Dan's dinner, my onion rings, then ordered a Big Kahuna Supersundae.

I shared that with her but she was still hungry, and her father and his loud friends were starting to annoy her so she took my hand and towed me out of the Busted Schooner.

As we walked through town the full moon was just coming up over the mountains and Kate wouldn't let go my hand. I asked her where we were headed.

"The deli," she said. "Gotta get something to eat."

"You already ate nine tons of food," I said. "I mean, I love food, but really. You should have seen how much you ate."

"I saw exactly. Now I want a banana split. Something to take my mind off how completely miserable everything got."

We got to the deli. It was shut down for the night and creepy dark inside. Spartacus was in the backyard, barking his head off.

"I feel as bad as you, Kate," I was saying. "Worse probably, since it's all my fault."

"Don't say that, Arron. It is not anybody's fault but McKraft's." She was searching through her key chain for the door key. It was dark and she took years to find it.

"I feel responsible," I said. "It's like that dumb egg test of Doc's. Like everything was just thrown at me all of sudden, too fast. And it's not my fault, but . . . but . . ."

"What but?" said Kate. "Arron! Where is that key?"

"But it is my fault because I feel responsible. I feel bad. I feel guilty—"

"QUIET, Spartacus!" Kate shouted. That dog would not shut up. He was barking like crazy, as if he were barking at something. . . .

"Don't you see, Kate?" I went on. "That's what the egg test was. I dropped the eggs. But it wasn't about me dropping anything, it was about the eggs breaking. It doesn't matter if it's not my fault, it's still my responsibility—"

"Here it is," said Kate, finally jamming the key into the lock.

"We gotta do something, Kate. We can't just sit here and let McKraft win like that. We have to do something."

As I said this, Kate opened the door and we stepped inside. She switched on the light, but it just flickered as it swung above the counter, and the room swam with moving shadows. She started to say, "That's strange," when we were hit by a cold blast of wind and the door slammed behind us.

"YOU DARN RIGHT YOU GOTTA DO SOME-THING!!" screamed a voice from somewhere behind the sushi counter.

I hit the dirt and went back against the wall, covering my ears.

In the sizzling lamplight, looming between the refrigerator and the vegetable juicer, Mama Kauai stared us down like some giant angry god. Her eyes were wide and red, her hair had flown out of its bun and hung down around her scowling face. She leveled her deadly cane at us like a shotgun. She had my attention.

"YOU GO!" said Mama Kauai. "YOU GO AND TELL THEM WHAT YOU DONE! TELL THEM WHAT YOU DONE GO AND DO!!"

"It's my fault, Mama Kauai," I shouted, cowering in the corner. "I'm sorry, really, I'll do anything you want—"

"SHUT UP!!!" she shouted. "YOU HAOLES TALK, TALK, TALK, KEEP TALKING. NOW SHUT UP. GO. GO NOW AND TELL THEM!! OR YOU HAVE MORE EVIL, ROTTEN, BAD-LUCK CURSES THAN EVER IN HISTORY!"

"Go where? Tell who?" cried Kate, who was on her knees and looking about as afraid as me.

"GO TO THE MENEHUNE. TELL THE MENEHUNE!" she shouted, then pop!—she shattered the light bulb with her cane and was gone.

CHAPTER *37*

"*I've got it!*" said Kate, as she finished her banana split. Her spoon dropped with a clink into the huge glass dish. "I don't know why I didn't think of this before."

She took down the chalkboard menu hanging over the counter and erased the day's specials. Then she took the colored chalk from the tray at the bottom of the board and began to draw very fast.

"What are you doing? Can't we get out of here?" I said.

"I'm drawing something," she said. She was concentrating hard, sticking her tongue out the side of her mouth. Her nose was dented in at the top again, the way I liked.

"What are you drawing?"

"I can't believe I was so stupid," she muttered. "I thought the map was important . . . "

"It is, I thought."

"Not the map itself, no. What is important is what the map says, where it can show you to get to."

"You're drawing the map?" I said.

"Yeah."

"No way you can just draw that map without looking at it."

"Arron, the whole time you were kidnapped I pored over that map. I stared at it for hours trying to get some clue. I thought maybe I'd figure out where they'd taken you to. I didn't figure out anything, of course, but I did pretty much memorize every crazy detail."

"Just pretty much?"

"Well, I think all of it, but I'm not perfect. Not all the time anyway," She smiled at me.

She finished working and stepped away from the drawing like she'd just done a Rembrandt, or something. I had to admit it looked just like the original to me. Kate was very proud of it. I started to realize what she had in mind.

"Wait a minute," I said. "Just one big fat minute. You're not thinking . . . You're not going to . . ."

"Well, yes, I am."

"You want to go into those caves? You want to go in there and tell a tribe of little elves that probably doesn't exist that you're very sorry for losing their map and a big bad man called McKraft is coming to build a hotel inside their volcano? That's what you want to do?"

"Mama said we have to. You heard her."

"This is nuts," I said. "You're actually going to do this? Right now?"

Kate nodded. "What happened to Mr. Brave 'we've-got-to-do-something-right-now' Pendleton?"

she said. "I thought you were all ready to take your share of the responsibility. To fight McKraft to the death."

"That's just it. Death. I'm afraid. What if McKraft is there now? What if we go in there, assuming we can even find a way, and McKraft is in there waiting for us?"

"I'm going, Arron. I've got to. You can come or not, but I have to try."

"Kate, what about my . . . Oh no, my parents! Do you realize what time it is? It's after midnight again! Do you have any idea how bad they are going to make my life now? I promised I'd see them tonight. It's not even tonight anymore, it's tomorrow!"

"Then it doesn't really matter how late you stay out, right?" said Kate.

"What are you talking about?"

"If you're already in trouble, you might as well stay to help me, then go get yelled at in the morning. Anyway, once they hear the story they'll understand. This is important."

"No, they will not understand, Kate. No one will understand. I don't even understand."

"I'm going, so you can do whatever you want."

There was a sad pause.

"Where?" I said.

"Where what?" muttered Kate.

"Where . . . where are we going?"

"You mean where am I going, don't you?"

"No." I sighed, remembering all the things Dr. Gomasio had told me. "Where are we going?"

By one o'clock Kate and I were on the ocean. She promised me she could drive a Zodiac and she seemed to handle the boat okay, but the water was rough. Luckily the moon was out—that was the only thing we had going for us.

"My dad won't mind," she had promised me, when we snuck into the hangar and hitched up his second-to-last Zodiac to her pickup truck. "I take the boats out all the time."

"At night?" I asked her.

"No. Not at night, exactly."

"I've got a bad feeling about this, Kate. I really do."

"There's nothing to worry about," she said. "I really know what I'm doing, I honestly do. I only wish—"

"What?! If you're wishing, then something's wrong."

"I just wish we could've seen Doc before doing this. To get his blessing, you know? For good luck."

"I think we're going to need a lot of it," I said.

"Well, we have some of his sushi," she said, patting her bag where she'd put the take-out tin of delicacies. "Hopefully that'll be luck enough. At least we can have a snack later."

Bouncing around in a rubber boat in the middle of the night was about the last place I'd want to eat anything, let alone raw fish and seaweed. Doc's sushi was kind of comforting, but I didn't see how useful it would be, unless we got lost in one of the sea caves and were starving to death.

It was windy and cold, so I took a sweatshirt out of my day-pack and put it on. That didn't help much when the waves smacked the boat, or when we smacked down hard into the water and got all splashed. It was hard going.

Once we lifted up on a really big wave—too big—and came smashing down like we'd hit concrete. My jaw flew up so hard I thought I cracked my teeth. Loose stuff was rolling over the rubber floor, snorkels and life vests and even a couple of fire extinguishers. Kate was calm but she got nicely sprayed, so she asked me to take the wheel while she put on a slicker and life vest.

"I can't!" I said. "I don't know how to drive one of these!"

"Arron, just keep the rudder straight, like this. You can't bump into anything out here—"

"I can't even drive a car!"

"It's easier than a car. Come on, I'm wet and freezing."

Finally I agreed.

"First put on a life vest," she said.

"This is crazy, Kate. Let's turn back."

"Honestly—you worry too much. Now put on the vest and come steer this boat."

I did like she said. I was totally scared crazy at first. It was like plunging into a big black nothingness. Bashing down off those waves every ten seconds made my brain crunch. Then Kate remembered to switch on the searchlight, which she should have done right away in the first place.

Now I could see a wedge of ocean, but the water was angry black. Anything could be lurking under the surface—a reef or whales or sharks . . .

"Hurry up! I don't like doing this," I said.

"Just a minute, I can't find my raincoat. Do you want me to find you one too?"

"Yes, but hurry." Then I saw the giant cliffs and mountains glowing eerily in the moonlight. They looked different at night, not green and friendly anymore.

"Kate! We're coming up on something!" I shouted. She was at the front of the raft, still fumbling around for her stuff.

"I think I can see some caves!"

She came quickly and took back the rudder. "Excuse me. Better find a good place and hang on."

"What? Is something wrong?"

"I don't know. Maybe." she said.

"What?!"

"We're being followed."

CHAPTER 38

Kate *headed directly for the cliffs.* They were huge and curved inward, like an ampitheater, like a whole chunk of the island had exploded off. There wasn't any beach; the cliffs dropped straight down to the sea and kept going, making the caves look like overgrown mouse holes in the giant wall.

Behind us I saw lights bouncing on the water. It looked as if three boats were in pursuit. They were a long way off but heading in our direction and going faster than we were. I didn't say anything. I thought if I opened my mouth, nothing would come out—except maybe I'd throw up. That banana split I ate was moving with a life all its own.

"Be ready to duck," called Kate, stopping the raft in front of the biggest cave. She kept checking over her shoulder, watching the waves and the other boats. They were getting closer. I could hear their engines now.

"Why did you stop?" I said.

"Gotta wait for a low point between the swells," she said, "otherwise we'll get smashed up on the roof of the cave entrance. See? Like that." She pointed as a big wave swelled up and covered the hole, filling the cave with water like a washing machine. "We don't want to be there when that happens."

"I don't think I want to be in there at all," I said. "So, are we turning back, or what?"

"Nope. Hold on tight!"

Kate gunned the engine and we slipped in very nicely, right between the swells, like she wanted. We tethered the raft, turned off the searchlight, and hid there for a while to see what those other boats were up to, but they never appeared. We figured they went to some other cave, or maybe they weren't really following us after all.

Once she thought it was safe, Kate turned the searchlight back on and started the engine. We rode around inside the cave, looking for clues. She had wrapped the chalkboard map in a garbage bag to keep the water off. Now she unwrapped it and studied it with her flashlight, following the red arrow as carefully as she could. But we kept ending up in the same dead end, a cave off the main tunnel, as big as a house.

"I give up," said Kate. She threw the flashlight down in frustration. "We looked every place there is. There aren't any secret passageways."

"Maybe we're not even in the right cave to begin with, Kate," I said. "Let's not get frustrated yet, okay? Let me see the board." I picked up the flashlight and studied it. "Where are we on here?"

"We're here," Kate said, pointing to a squiggly line on the map. "But that can't be right. There's a mistake."

"Why?"

"Well, see that red arrow?"

"Yeah."

"That's where we're supposed to go, but it's impossible to do that. There's a wall there. The arrow points in that exact direction—I even checked the compass—but there's no place to go, is there? It's solid rock."

I had to admit it looked like a dead end, but since we'd come this far, we made one more careful search. After fifteen minutes of circling, I wondered how to make Kate give up and go home. That's when we found the passage.

The far wall of the cave sloped back at the water's edge, and from a few yards away it looked like solid wall. But up close we saw that there was a space a few feet high leading back into the darkness. Just enough to slip the Zodiac under if we both lay down and Kate steered without looking, which is what we did.

The passageway got narrower and tighter till I thought we'd get wedged in there for good. But after thirty feet or so of genuine misery, the crevice opened and we found ourselves inside another big cave.

It was spooky. This cave's walls had a wild glow that sparkled in our flashlight beam and shimmered from the ripples on the water. This cave was bigger. Rivers of what must have been fresh water poured out from holes in the wall, crashed together, foamed, and bounced away into the twists and turns of a dozen small tunnels.

"Cool," I said. "Now let's get out of here."

"Just a little farther," said Kate. "Let me check the map again."

"I think we've come plenty far." Suddenly I was feeling weird, as if I were being watched. "I never told anyone this, but along with spiders and getting buried alive, small tunnels and stuff really make me uncomfortable. Are you listening, Kate?"

"I am trying to concentrate."

"Kate, I don't think we should be here. I have a funny feeling. Not funny haha, funny bad, Kate. Really. I don't think we're supposed to be here. Kate? Listen, I'm serious. I have a bad feeling."

"There's nothing to worry about, Arron," she said. "I know just what I'm doing. Nothing's going to happen."

"Kate, I want to go. Let's make our apologies to the Menehune right here and go. This is a good place for it—"

"Arron! Come on now, just a little farther. I know what I'm doing, I promise. Besides this is exciting—"

I was about to say that she couldn't know too much about what she was doing if no human being had ever come out of here alive—or even dead for that matter, when—

BUMP!

Something hit us.

The raft was bumped out of the water about a foot and Kate's map went over the side, the chalk dissolving as it sank to the bottom.

"Well that's great! That's just great!" said Kate, sounding like her father. "Now what are we supposed to do?!"

"We're going to turn around," I said. "Right now."

"But—"

"Turn the boat around! Didn't you feel that bump?"

"I thought that was you."

"Me?" I said. "I'm serious, get us out of here!"

"What's the big problem?"

"There is something alive in here with us! There is something underneath the boat!"

"There is not something under the boat, Arron," scolded Kate. "You're getting hysterical. Just relax."

"I felt something. I am not kidding around here."

"There's nothing here, Arron, I promise. The passageway is too small for anything except . . . "

but Kate's voice trailed off uneasily.

"What? WHAT?" I shouted.

"How do you feel about sharks," she said.

CHAPTER 39

Kate *was gunning the engine,* trying to turn us around so we could get back to the crevice, when the shark came and bit our propeller off. He got a good grip on the bottom of the propeller shaft and started yanking and twisting at it, shaking the raft and sending half our belongings over the side.

The stern yanked under, the bow popped up, and I slid toward the mangled engine and the monster shark head chomping its way on up the back of the raft. It happened too fast to be scared, I was concentrating too hard on scrambling my feet away from its toothy mouth.

"Arron!" screamed Kate. "Hit it with something! Bang it on the nose!"

I grabbed the metal first-aid box and whacked him, but it only seemed to make him hungrier. He was shaking the engine like a rag until it was smoking and grinding and useless. We had to do something or he'd eat through the boat till he got to us.

Kate pulled me into the prow. We huddled together and waited for the shark to bite the right place and pop the air out of the Zodiac. He was taking a breather now, still hanging on with his teeth, but not moving. His eyes were black and cold like death.

"I heard stories about this," gasped Kate, "about Mo'o, the shark god who guards all the sacred places. But I never took them literally."

"Well, this is literally happening," I said. "What do we DO?! Why is he just sitting there, looking at us? Soon he's gonna bite right into the boat. You know that, don't you? We'll explode!"

"He stopped. Maybe he'll get bored and go away."

With that, the shark shook its head, ripped the engine completely off, and started chewing the rubber floor.

We were drifting dangerously close to the biggest of the rivers pouring from the wall, getting caught in its fast current. It crashed and bashed its way over jagged rocks and dips, spraying foam and leading deep into who knew what bad, dark places.

We had no map.

We had no weapons.

All we had was a day-pack full of dirty clothes, a killer shark, and twenty pieces of sushi—

"The sushi!" said Kate.

"You're hungry?"

"NO, throw him the sushi!"

I found the box in the mess on the floor and

grabbed a handful of the stuff and threw it. Some of it bounced off the sharks nose. He went wild. With just one sniff, he snapped it up and dove to catch the pieces he missed.

He loved it! Soon he was back, swimming around and begging for more, like a big dog.

It wasn't likely we'd find a better use for Doc's sushi, so I pitched the rest of it far out into the water. The monster watched it fly, then took off like a bullet to snap up his first gourmet meal. By the time he started back to us, we were getting sucked far down into one of the river tunnels. I watched him swim slowly back and forth till we disappeared into the twisting rapids.

The current was rough. We bashed against the wall, then spun around, rushed into some rocks, spun the other way, and kept bouncing and crashing and spinning deep into the maze of tunnels.

I clung to the ropes, terrified that I would bounce out of the raft and into the cold water, or that Kate would—leaving me alone to be sucked down into the deepest cave in the universe and die. I could deal with the dying part, but the being alone part would not be good.

"Duck!" cried Kate as we rushed under an overhanging bridge of stone. It nearly scalped me—I felt my hair go whoosh against the lava rock.

"How ya' doing?"

"F-f-fine," I said. "You?"

"Hanging in there." She was having fun! "Don't worry! We're gonna be oookay."

The river finally slowed down to a meandering stream, and we drifted to rest on a sandy bank. It was amazing we'd kept afloat at all. There were countless ugly gashes and scars on the Zodiac, all of them looking about ready to burst. The raft was useless. We left it and slowly started walking. Kate tried drawing the map in the sand, but she did a lousy job and gave up, saying she didn't remember anything about getting out anyway.

We didn't need a flashlight since the walls still glowed in that eerie way—all green and murky, but bright enough to see by. It kept us from tripping over any stalagmites and busting a leg. We kept along the side of the stream when we could, but usually we had to splash through it, always on the lookout for a passage leading up and out. Everything was wet and slimy, and there were strange white crabs in the water that tried to pinch through our sneakers.

We walked for a while before Kate found a spot she liked. It was a round cavern, jagged with crystals, some of them giant, the size of boulders and telephone poles.

"This will do," she said, sitting down on a sandy patch and taking some things out of her pack—an apple, two granola bars and some smooth river stones. She stacked all this up into a little pyramid in front of her.

"I wish we still had some of that sushi," she said. "That would have been perfect."

"Don't you think we should keep moving? What if we run out of oxygen, or something?"

"We can't run out of oxygen, silly. Worst that would happen is we'd starve to death. Unless those crabs are good raw. . . . "

"Forget it, no way," I said. "Can I have one of those granola bars?"

"No. This is an offering to the Menehune. A gift so that they forgive us for trespassing and losing the map and everything."

Then she began talking to the thin, musty air, just as if someone else were listening besides me.

"Hello," she called. "Ummm, I'm Katherine Pierce, daughter of Alisa Nonohe and Captain Daniel Pierce and this is Arron Pendleton, son of— what are your parents' first names?" she asked me.

"David and Judy," I said. "Listen, why don't—"

"Son of David and Judy Pendleton from New York," she continued. "This is his first visit to Kauai, but he's been through a lot. He's almost not a haole anymore. Anyway, we're really, really sorry for barging down on you like this, without warning, or invitation, but—"

"Kate, this is crazy!"

"SHHH! Don't pay attention to Arron. Mama Kauai sent us. She says she knows you. Anyway, she told us to tell you that we were really stupid to lose your map and that now this big rotten jerk has it and he's planning to build a big, rotten hotel right down here in your sacred home. Actually, he wants you to build it for him, which is ridiculous, of course.

"His name is Lewis B. McKraft. I don't know his parents' names, but whatever you do, whatever he says, don't trust him, don't make any deals with him. I don't know if you've been outside lately, but the island's changing and it's only going to get worse if he has anything to do with it. So, uh, that's it, that's why we came. You have anything to say, Arron?"

"No. I don't. I think we should go now."

We started moving again.

We found pathways carved into the rock, some leading up steep slopes to sharp ledges. It was warm, like you could feel the lava heating the rocks from miles below. I got more and more desperate to see the outside world, even just a sliver of moonlight.

"What are the chances of a rescue party?" I asked.

"For us? I don't think any chance at all. Nobody knows we're gone yet. We didn't tell anybody we were going, or where, or anything, so don't get your hopes up."

"What if McKraft's down here?"

"Try not to think about it."

"Oh, God, this is horrible. I can't believe this is happening! Kate, if you don't know what you're doing I can take it, I'll understand, but I need to know if you honestly know what to do."

"Sure," she said, like she completely could not understand why I was concerned. "We just keep going up."

So that's what we did, and it went pretty well, just climbing and passing through all these amazing shining passageways. Sometimes it was so pretty I forgot to be scared; sometimes it was even fun, in a scary sort of way . . . until I tripped over the dead body.

It lay there with one hand stretched out for help, the other . . . with a shock, I saw there was no other hand! It had been chopped off at the wrist. This was the body of Alistair Courtenay Vaneblone III! It looked like he'd been crawling around in here for quite some time before he died, which did not fill me with a feeling of hope and joy. His Bulwer Academy sweatshirt was torn and eaten by crabs. He was extremely dead, very bony, and shriveled. His color was a green I had never known existed.

"I thought we might find him down here," said Kate. "Only I had hoped he might be alive."

"This is so disgusting I can't deal with it," I said, squirming into a corner and trying not to look at the body. "Please, please, can we sit down and start screaming for help. We haven't tried that yet—"

"Quiet!" said Kate.

She cupped her hand against her ear.

"What?"

"SHHH!"

I listened too. There was something, some sound in some faraway cave. A prickly cold ran up my spine and into my hair.

It sounded like . . . music. . . .

"A—B—C—D—E—F—G—H—I got a girl in Kalamazoo. I don't want to boast, but I know she's the toast of Kalamazoo zoo zoo zoo zoo zoo."

It was an old big band tune that my grandparents might have listened to.

"Years have gone by, my my how she grew . . . "

"Glenn Miller, 1943," said Kate. She might have known all about jazz, but she still seemed as completely surprised as me to be hearing it inside a dormant volcano.

"Come on, let's find where it's coming from!" she said. I had to race to follow her.

The passageway got narrow and harder to climb. A hot wind was rushing by, and it carried that ridiculous song along with it, getting louder

220

the higher we climbed. Ahead of me, Kate wormed herself through a tight squeeze and suddenly disappeared. I panicked and started to run, catching my pack on a sharp finger of lava stone. The whole side of it ripped apart, sending my belongings spilling every which way—my toothbrush, my shampoo, my dirty clothes, and all the dozens of brochures I'd collected that first day at the tourist information desk. All the stupid, glossy, sell-out, plastic hula-show advertisements hit that hot wind and took off, flapping like multicolored bats. The tunnel was a whirlwind of paper.

"Arron, where are you? What are you doing?" called Kate.

I couldn't explain. I tried my best to grab what I could, but most of the flyers and brochures were blown away into dozens of other dark holes. I squeezed past that tight spot and found Kate staring through a chink in the wall, a chink that overlooked a deadly drop into some ancient gully.

"We've had it now," she said, sounding unusually grave.

"Oh, no," I said. "What? What?"

"One guess."

"McKraft? Oh, God, he's here?! Does he know we're here?"

"Look for yourself."

I looked.

Sure enough, down below was McKraft and all

his nasty friends, all the ones I'd met and some new ones too. They had Zodiacs tethered in the stream. They had guns and flashlights and spelunking equipment, ropes, backpacks, and even a big stereo playing McKraft's favorite big band selections. McKraft stood there smiling and waving up at us, while all my brochures floated down on them like moths and snowflakes.

"Do you have a reservation?" said a snickering voice behind us. We turned to see a slimier-than-usual Slimy Jack aiming a pistol from his hip.

We were caught.

Chapter *40*

K*ate and I were tied together* with bungee cords and brought down. There was no chance of escape. This big cave was evidently where McKraft planned to build his casino. Banners were strung from stalactites with big red letters announcing:

COMING SOON!
PELE HOTEL & CONDOMINIUMS!!

There were also plenty of no trespassing signs posted, as if anyone would actually stumble down here by accident.

Slimy Jack tried to start up a conversation, but I said something rude so he just threw us down onto the sand. He went off to get his boss, telling us not to go anywhere, which was moronic seeing that we were tied back-to-back and unable to even sit up.

Next thing I knew, McKraft was standing over us, grinning, his ridiculous miner's-helmet light beaming down off his head and blinding me. I was struggling to see anyway, since I had sand in my eye. It was also hard to breathe, the bungee cords had been wrapped so tight.

"What a wonderful surprise." He laughed. "All the way down here, now that's what I call enterprising. May I be so bold as to ask what you are doing?"

"It's a free country last time I looked," snapped Kate.

"I most heartily agree with that," said McKraft, reminding me how free he was to murder us in cold blood, without anyone finding out. He seemed very happy. Something jingled in his hand, like keys or money.

"Want to know why I'm here?" he asked.

"Like I don't know already," said Kate.

"You only know part of it, Miss Pierce. Shall I tell you, Mr. Pendleton?"

"If you feel you must," I muttered.

Out of his hand he dropped a stream of jangling things that sparkled and thudded into the sand.

They were coins. Gold coins.

"You can keep those as a memento," said McKraft. "There's enough left for me, don't worry."

"Gold?" said Kate and me.

"Gold. Emeralds. Diamonds. Silver. Not to mention all the natural mineral deposits. All that good stuff. Buried treasure."

"What? You mean real treasure?" I said, kind of excited by the sound of that. "Whose is it? I mean, where'd it come from?"

"There's no buried treasure here," snapped Kate.

"There's always buried treasure, Miss Pierce. It's an essential ingredient. Besides, how do you think I was going to finance my hotel? You didn't actually believe all that garbage about the Menehune, did you? You didn't actually think all that sad mumbo jumbo was to be taken seriously? I hoped you would have learned from your mother's mistakes."

"You don't know what you're saying," stammered Kate. "You're going to be very sorry." She was upset. My back being against hers, I felt her get kind of trembly, as if she were trying not to cry.

"So I hit a nerve, did I? I guess I didn't realize how attached you'd become to the idea of those magical little buggers, Miss Pierce."

"You're lying!" said Kate, crying now. "The Menehune are real, and they'll never let you get away with this! I told them all about you, I warned them—"

"They're a fantasy!" McKraft shouted and laughed. "A stupid children's story! A JOKE! I only brought them into it so nobody would guess that there was all this glorious, beautiful treasure. The stuff's been here for more than three hundred years. Mr. Pendleton, you're a smart boy. These islanders will believe anything, but I'm surprised that you would."

"Fine. Whatever," I said. "Whose treasure is it?"

"MINE," boomed McKraft.

"Before you," I said. "Where did it come from?"

"We don't have all night, but I do just love this story. Gather 'round the fire and I'll tell you. A long, long time ago, a British admiral in the Royal Navy mutinied and became a pirate, looting his brother officer's trade ships. And since he knew all the trade routes and secrets of the British government, he became a very successful pirate indeed. His name was Alistair Vaneblone the first, and when he became an old pirate, he hid his loot in the darkest, hardest-to-find spot in all the Pacific— the bowels of a tiny island called Kauai. He was here before Captain Cook, but since he was a pirate, the British didn't want to admit that. So they sent Cook on a trade run to these islands, but actually it was a secret mission to bring back

Vaneblone and all his gold. Cook never found it, and he died trying. You following me? Am I going too fast?"

"No," I said, entranced by the story of adventure. "What happened next?"

"Nothing. Not for three hundred years, until Vaneblone's family papers were released to his great-great-great-grandson Alistair the third, our handless friend. He was working for me at the time, while I was in London financing my Blue Egret Hotel. I got wind of the map, but the boy up and quit me before we had a proper good-bye—the greedy little snot. Anyway, I followed his trail for years, till I caught up with him back on Kauai. The rest is history in the making, and you're part of it! Doesn't that make you happy?"

"Yeah, kinda," I said.

"NO! It's not true," cried Kate, but she was sobbing and couldn't say anymore.

"Well." McKraft sighed "It's sad, but we all have to grow up at some point and say bye-bye to all the dreams of youth. So, Mr. Pendleton, I expect you're feeling right silly about now."

"Why should I?" I said, trying to sound hard as nails.

"First because you had the chance to be my partner and get rich, but instead you got tied up with the most pathetic characters in the South Seas. And second, because now I'm going to have

226

you both thrown into a pit of boiling lava. There's a perfect one nearby."

I went to kick him in the shins, but I couldn't move my legs. So I tried biting his foot instead. He stepped away just before I could chomp him.

"Don't make it more unpleasant for yourself than it's got to be, Mr. Pendleton," he said. "We'll be heading out fairly soon. Someone will come to collect you."

Then he walked off toward the river, where his treasure was being loaded up. I tried talking to Kate but she couldn't say a thing, she was crying so hard.

No one came to give us food or water, or to check if we were still alive—but then why would they if they were just going to throw us into boiling lava? There was the sound of shuffling feet, of workers hauling, and over this McKraft's voice shouting orders. We managed to prop ourselves up against some big crystals, and from this angle we could see McKraft and his loot.

There was tons of it. Actual buried treasure!

McKraft's men filed out of the tunnels with bags, boxes, trunks, sacks, and wheelbarrows of it. It was the real thing. It was piled on the ground in a heap, and then loaded into the Zodiacs or nailed into crates. All the while still more of it was hauled out of the tunnels by the goons. This was the horde of all time. There were chests swimming with gold—bricks, coins, and medallions. There were silver plates and mountains of rubies and emeralds, some the size of marbles, some like gum balls. There were swords and muskets and cannons, with ceremonial cannonballs of solid jade. Goblets and jewelry, crowns and rings—all of it shining there in one place. Enough booty for every pirate ship that ever sailed in the history of pirates.

So this was it, I thought. From the very beginning, it had all been about treasure. I knew I was probably supposed to feel let down like Kate was, but I was too overwhelmed. I was thrilled by the whole smell of adventure, until I remembered that unless Kate or I came up with a very bright idea very soon, we'd both be part of history the way the Vaneblones were.

I was trying to think of something brave to say to Kate, the way you always see the hero in a movie say something smart or funny, when she sat up stiffly, wrinkled her nose, and sniffed the air.

"What? What are you doing?" I asked.

"I smell something. Do you smell anything all of a sudden?"

"I have sand in my nose," I said, trying to inhale and then sneezing violently. "Excuse me."

"I thought I smelled . . . cigars," she said.

"Arron, I think we're going to be okay."

It seemed like hours had gone by until Slimy Jack came back with Vance Viebermann. They carried us to where McKraft stood, ready with his climbing gear. Now he had on one of those Tyrolean hats—like he was about to climb the Alps. There was a feather in its brim, and it was tilted back at a jaunty angle. It clashed with the red texas barbecue apron he wore.

He took a sloppy bite from a hot dog impaled on a long, pronged fork.

"Not done enough, Bruno," he said, handing the wienie over to one of his goons. "A few more seconds over the pit." Then he turned to us. "We're going on a little hike now, kids," he said. "If you prefer, we can keep you tied up and carry you, or you can walk by yourselves. That would be nicer for us, since we have some of that treasure to carry—I'm taking the most valuable crates with me. You'll have to promise not to run away."

"What do you want, Kate?" I asked her.

"I want to walk."

"We're walking."

"What brave little soldiers we are," sneered McKraft. "Well, let's move. I've got golf at eleven."

We trekked up over the river and into distant, snaking catacombs. A few guys were left with the Zodiacs, but nearly twenty men followed McKraft. They carried all the equipment, plus the massive, heavy crates of treasure. I don't know how they managed it.

McKraft didn't carry anything, of course, but he did ask us if we wouldn't mind carrying something since there was so much stuff. Kate told him to sit on it. Actually, she said something worse, but I don't think I should repeat it.

The tunnels wound around every which way. There was no telling where we were, only that we were going deeper and deeper into the twisted puzzle. McKraft was the only one who knew now; he had the map. Even if Kate and I could escape, we'd never find our way out. I wasn't able to talk to Kate without being overheard, but I was curious why she seemed suddenly confident ever since smelling the cigar smoke.

It had been like a sign to her. I racked my brain—cigars, cigars . . . then I remembered. Mama Kauai smoked cigars!

I squeezed Kate's hand. My hand was sweaty, but so was hers. Please, I thought, please help us, Mama Kauai. I'm sorry I ever doubted you.

The going was rough. Twice we came to holes in the trail. The men put boards down so we could cross and so they could slide the crates carefully to the other side. Some passageways were so filled with stalagmites and stalactites that we could barely get through. No one talked.

Then, far down, in the basement of the earth, the tunnel opened up into a cavern and I suddenly smelled lava. I don't know how I knew what lava smelled like, but I knew. The place was roaring with waterfalls and steam and there was a murky, red glow ahead in the darkness. This was it. If whoever was going to save us didn't do it right now, it would be too late.

"Be careful where you step," said McKraft, as we headed up a particularly narrow ledge. "It's wet and you don't want to slip down into the water-falls."

"Thanks, boss," said Slimy Jack.

"What do you care where I step," said Kate. It sounded like she was trying to pick a fight. "What difference does it possibly make now?"

"Just being courteous, Miss Pierce," said McKraft.

"Very funny." She laughed. "Watch your step—then shove us into a volcano. What a comedian! You're a totally ridiculous man."

"Shut up!" said Slimy Jack.

I squeezed her hand tight.

"Oh, what are you gonna do?" she said. "Get mad? Yell at me? I'm soo scared—"

Don't start, Kate, I thought, don't make this worse than it is.

"Hey, shut up! I mean it," said Jack again.

We were so near the lava I could feel its heat on my skin. Don't do anything stupid, Kate, I thought. We still may have a chance, just don't blow it.

"If I wasn't a pacifist I'd throw YOU in a volcano!" she yelled.

"I'm trying to do this as pleasantly as possible, Miss Pierce. If you don't like it, why don't you keep it to yourself. And don't get any clever notions about escaping down any of these water tunnels. You can't get away n—OW!!"

In the semidarkness, I could see him clutch his head and fall on his butt.

"Who threw that?! Who threw that rock?!" he shouted.

The next instant, there were rocks flying everywhere—sailing through the air, cracking off the walls, knocking people square in their eyes. The men were shouting and sliding and falling on the slippery ledge.

"We're under attack!" shouted Slimy Jack.

"I can see that, you idiot, but WHO? WHO is attacking us?!" McKraft was hysterical with rage. "NO ONE can BE HERE!"

Kate and I ducked and huddled together, our arms pulled over our heads to shield us from the flying rocks. So far we hadn't been hit.

"Are we being rescued?"

"Yes!" she said.

"By who?"

"By THEM!"

McKraft was screaming and waving his arms at the walls and ceiling. "NO, it's not possible! You're not real! YOU DON'T EXIST!"

I thought he'd flipped his cookies, but then I saw dark shadows with big green cat eyes racing down on us, chattering and laughing. Little things, running up, down, sideways, zipping like geckos over the cave. They poured up from steaming cracks in the floor, scurried out of the water tunnels—hundreds, thousands, I don't know how many cat-eyed things.

Men were dropping their guns and backpacks, running, falling, howling in fear. They dropped the crates of treasure. I heard rumblings from the lava pit. The ground shook. I thought, OH GEEZ, this volcano is going to blow! But it didn't. It just shook us off the ledge forcing us to slide down toward the black holes and the water.

Some rescue, I thought! The Menehune are real, they show up at the last moment, and now we're going to die quicker than before! Everything was completely crazy.

Men were sliding past me into the water holes. Everywhere I looked the tiny Menehune swarmed, jumping from the ceiling, biting, kicking, wrestling.

Above us, McKraft was still screaming. He was desperately trying to hold the biggest crate against the wall, but with every rumble of the earth, the crate inched farther away.

"HELP ME, DAMMIT!" he shouted. "MY TREASURE! YOU DON'T KNOW HOW BADLY I WANT THIS!"

These were the last words anyone heard him say. The crate wobbled off the ledge and slid like a torpedo toward the falls, L. B. McKraft hugging the front end and screaming all the way. Down it went, zipping over the wet floor, zipping into a water tunnel, and smashing to bits—with old L.B. mushed against the rocks like the inside of an Oreo.

Suddenly I lost my grip and fell. Kate was gone. I slipped backward into a whirlwind of water, watching the Menehune race and laugh and wink their green cat eyes.

CHAPTER *41*

I *woke up with my head spinning* and my stomach rolling. The sun beat on my eyelids, causing an awful pounding inside my brain. Someone splashed cold water on my face.

"Wake up, Arron. Come on, you can do it," said a voice that sounded like Kate's.

"We're out?" I mumbled. "We're safe?"

"We're out and safe."

"The Menehune . . . McKraft is dead, right? I was drowning. . . . The Menehune are real, Kate."

"I know. Can you sit up?"

I sat up.

"Where are we?"

"In a Zodiac, off Haena Beach. Don't ask me how, or why, but the Menehune must have saved us. I don't think any of the others made it, though."

I looked around at the beach and the sunshine. "Holy smoke," I said. "It's good to be alive. I think I'm going to throw up."

Two other Zodiacs were tied to the one we lay in. They were the rafts McKraft had brought down into the caves.

"What are they doing here—"

"I'm not asking any questions. They're ours now," said Kate. "Those rafts are going to save my dad's business." She sat up and shook some sand out of her hair. "Can you move? We should try to get back to town. Everyone must be worried sick by now."

There was no gas in the Zodiacs, so we slowly paddled to the shore and tethered them to some trees. Then we hitchhiked over to Hanalei in the back of some farmer's old pickup truck. He dropped us off at the Tropical Deli and we walked in there expecting to catch heck, when what do you know? We got cheers and applause. Everyone was there, I mean everybody—Captain Dan, Dr.

Gomasio, Craig, Joanne, Terry, Sammy, Spartacus, not to forget Mama Kauai and her big family—everyone crammed in that little rickety deli, eating sushi and slurping down mango shakes with big, goofy grins.

It seems both Doc and Mama knew we were all right. Don't ask how, just one of those things. They'd been assuring everybody, especially Captain Dan, that we were fine and bound to come through the door any second. Dan was desperately relieved to see his daughter and me, giving us hugs and kisses and snuffling back tears because he was embarrassed to cry. Instead, he grabbed a tuft of my hair and said, "You didn't do anything ungentlemanly with my daughter down there in those caves, did you?"

He was only kidding, but I turned ten shades of red and Kate punched him hard in the arm.

Then it was story time. We described everything that happened to us. They were all amazed. Everyone especially loved the part about McKraft getting crushed by his own crate of treasure.

At this Mama Kauai snorted with pleasure, puffing on her familiar-smelling cigar.

Then Dan hitched up his shorts and told us the news from town. It was nearly as exciting.

"You're not gonna believe this," he said, "but Stingray Cruises is no more. Both their office and their hangar were demolished some time during the night. I mean tortilla time. Flattened—like by a tornado. Only nothing else was hit."

"Never seen anything so beautiful before," said Doc.

"Yes, it was pretty perfect," said Dan.

"Menehune done go and busted up all whatever McKraft ever touch," said Mama Kauai. "For good his land has big-time curse. You make me proud, children."

"Thank you," said Kate.

"Do you believe what Mama say now, boy? Do you believe the Menehune got big time, powerful ho'okalakupua?"

"Yes, Mama," I said.

"Next time, you believe Mama Kauai? Next time you listen mo' better what she tells you?"

"Yes, Mama," I said again, trying not to blush. "I promise."

Everyone was still laughing, and having a party almost, when the door swung open and a very oddlooking group of people stood there, staring at us. They wore lots of mismatched clothes and carried eleven suitcases. They looked tired. They looked angry.

"Well, young man, I hope you have a very, very good explanation," said my father.

"Dad!" I said. "Mom!" I said.

"We know we're your parents," snapped my mother. "What we don't know is where the devil you were last night."

"I, um . . . I . . . " was all I managed.

Captain Dan stepped forward with confidence, putting a robust hand out to shake with my father.

"You must be Mr. Pendleton!" he cried. "Sir, let me introduce myself. Captain Daniel Pierce. Kate's my daughter. I've been kind of looking after your son, who by the way is the finest young man I've ever had the pleasure to know."

"Hi. Nice to meet you," mumbled my father, putting down his suitcases and shaking hands.

"What're you all doing in the doorway?" said Doc. "Come in, have something to eat. You look pretty tired."

"Yeah, absolutely, come in!" said Captain Dan. "What are you doing carrying all that luggage?"

"Our hotel . . . you tell them, honey," said my father, looking harshly at me.

"Our hotel . . . the Blue Egret . . . ran into a few difficulties," she said.

"What kind of difficulties?" asked Kate, brightly.

"Maybe we all should sit down," sighed my father. "Let's all just sit and then everybody can explain to me just what the heck is going on on this island."

*   *   *

238

So it happened that for my last few days on Kauai, my whole family had to move in with Captain Dan. This was because the Blue Egret Hotel had been pretty much destroyed in the night, sending the guests into a frenzy. No one could stay in the hotel now, not with thousands of rats, mongooses, lizards, and bugs sharing the place with them. Plus, the pool had mysteriously filled with hot tar and a horrible stench had started to seep into all the rooms. Then at about five in the morning the fiberglass volcano in the driveway erupted, oozing real lava into the lobby. The Blue Egret had to shut down.

The Menehune had won.

Eventually my parents did come to believe my story. There were too many people backing me up for them not to. And eventually they even got used to living with Captain Dan. They had no choice. There wasn't a free room anywhere else on the island. It was real cramped with Mom and Dad, Lisa, Robby, Tracy, and me all crashing in the living room, sleeping where we could find space. But Dan was very hospitable, and I think they grew to like it.

And finally I got my vacation. I took long walks with Kate on the north shore beaches, swam in silver tide pools, and watched the fish go by. Spartacus always came with us, guarding us from dangers that never came, and Kauai was saved from its evil spirits, at least for a while.

I was pretty broken up when we had to leave, packing off to my old life. I went by the deli to say good-bye to Doc. He was busy chopping like always, but he found time to cheer me up. He gave me a present he'd been keeping for me—a little egg carved out of Hawaiian koa wood.

"This is your egg, Arron san," he said. "You're responsible. Understand?"

I nodded.

"You'll always have a home in Kauai," he said. "You helped save her and she won't forget that, Arron san. She is safe, for now. But soon there will be other things to be done, new battles to fight. You must be responsible. If you like, I will call you when it's time."

"Thanks," I said. "I'll be waiting."

My parents were also waiting, waiting to go to the airport. Kate walked me back to her house from the deli. I was too miserable to say good-bye. It was the last thing on earth I wanted to do, but Kate was whistling happily.

"You're not going to miss me, are you," I said.

"Sure I am, what are you talking about?" she asked.

"You're whistling. I'm leaving in a half hour and you're whistling."

She didn't stop.

"Gee, I mean, who knows when I'll be back. It could be a long time."

"Not too long," she said.

"Are you sure?" I asked, hopeful.

"Pretty sure," she said, and smiled.

"I'll call you," I said.

"You will?"

"Yes. And I'll write to you too. But I'll call."

"It's expensive from New York," she said.

"I know, but I have to. I can get a job to pay for it—and for my next trip out. I'll get a job at a deli, maybe."

"Your job at the Tropical will be waiting."

There was a pause, and then she said, "I have an idea. Something we can work on."

"What?"

She turned and faced me, looking right in my eyes.

"Okay," she said. "Try and guess what I'm thinking."

"I can't do that," I said.

"Just try. If we get good at this, maybe you can cut down on phone bills. Now, what am I thinking?"

I looked at her for a long time, imagining how much I'd miss her, realizing she was really the best friend I ever had.

"I think I love you," I said, without realizing it.

Her eyes lit up. "You did it!" she said. "That was what I was thinking."

"Now you read my mind," I said.

She closed her eyes, concentrating. "You want to kiss me?"

"Yeah," I said. Then I kissed her.

"Tell them all I'll see them soon," I said.

"Who all?"

"Everybody. Your dad, Doc, Mama Kauai. You. Tell them I promise. Tell them . . . Captain Hawaii *will* return."

ABOUT THE AUTHOR

Anthony Dana Arkin is a screenwriter and an actor. Captain Hawaii is his first novel. He was born in New York City and raised in Westchester County, NY. He currently lives in Los Angeles, CA.